His whole body had gone into shock the minute Annie stepped out of the kitchen.

She had blossomed from a pretty girl into a stunner. Seeing her again had made him feel weak and needy.

He despised weakness, particularly in himself. His childhood and the military had taught him that. Be strong. Be tough. Never let them see you sweat.

Encountering Annie had made him sweat.

Over the years the girl he'd been crazy about as a teen had lingered in his mind. A turn of phrase, a song on the radio, a woman with high cheekbones could start the memories flowing fast and painful.

She was none too happy to see him, either, but she had good reason. What she didn't know was that his reasons for leaving all those years ago were every bit as good as her reasons to despise him. He hadn't told her then, and he sure wouldn't tell her now why he'd had to leave Redemption.

He sighed. Protection was his business. He'd loved Annie enough to protect her at eighteen.

He'd protect her now with his silence.

Books by Linda Goodnight

Love Inspired

In the Spirit of...Christmas
A Very Special Delivery
*A Season for Grace
*A Touch of Grace
*The Heart of Grace
Missionary Daddy
A Time to Heal
Home to Crossroads Ranch
The Baby Bond
**Finding Her Way Home
**The Wedding Garden

*The Brothers' Bond
**Redemption River

LINDA GOODNIGHT

Winner of a RITA® Award for excellence in inspirational fiction, Linda Goodnight has also won the Booksellers' Best, ACFW Book of the Year and a Reviewers' Choice Award from *RT Book Reviews*. Linda has appeared on the Christian bestseller list and her romance novels have been translated into more than a dozen languages. Active in orphan ministry, this former nurse and teacher enjoys writing fiction that carries a message of hope and light in a sometimes dark world. She and husband, Gene, live in Oklahoma. Readers can write to her at linda@lindagoodnight.com, or c/o Steeple Hill Books, 233 Broadway, Suite 1001, New York, NY 10279.

The Wedding Garden
Linda Goodnight

Steeple
Hill®

Published by Steeple Hill Books™

STEEPLE HILL BOOKS

Steeple
Hill®

ISBN-13: 978-0-373-87595-5

THE WEDDING GARDEN

Copyright © 2010 by Linda Goodnight

www.SteepleHill.com

Printed in U.S.A.

You will know the truth,
and the truth will set you free.
—*John* 8:32

To my cousin Kay, for prayers, kind words,
and for literally going the extra mile during
a very difficult time. Thanks, "Susie."

Prologue

There was a man in the house. Again.

Sloan's stomach got that funny, sick feeling like he was going to vomit. He hated when Mama brought someone home at night. Someone drunk and noisy. He knew what people said about her. Joni Hawkins was no good, like her jailbird husband. They gossiped, said dirty things about her. He was eleven. He wasn't stupid. He knew what the words meant.

They were all big fat liars.

He tiptoed down the dark hallway to the door, careful not to be heard. Mama would tell him to go back to bed. But he worried when she brought a man home.

He could hear them in there, but he couldn't make out the words. The man's voice rumbled, rising at times. Then Mama's soothing tones would calm him down. She was good at soothing.

A narrow beam of light sliced along the edge of the wooden floor. Breath held, he placed his right eye against the skinny crack and slowly, slowly let the air ease out through his nose.

He couldn't see much. A flash of Mama's pink diner shirt. A man's leg in dark pants. Dress-up pants. Sloan could see a big hand, too, held out toward Mama as though asking for something.

What was that on the man's wrist? A watch? Sloan squeezed closer until the wood pressed hard into his face and his eyelashes folded back against his eyelid. Not a watch, a fancy bracelet with stones. Sloan held back a laugh, relaxing a little. Only a sissy would wear a bracelet like a girl. Who was in there?

"Mama?" he said before he could stop the word.

The voices inside the room stilled. Footsteps moved toward him. The door cracked open the tiniest bit and Mama's face appeared.

"What are you doing up, Sloan?"

"Who's in there with you?"

"Nobody important. Go back to bed. You have school tomorrow."

More curious now than worried, he made no effort to leave. Mama reached out and smoothed his hair. "On my next day off, we'll go fishing. Just me and you. Okay?"

When he nodded, his mama smiled. Then she shut the door.

He never saw her again.

Chapter One

Sloan Hawkins killed the purring Harley beneath the cool shade of a swaying willow, lowered the kickstand and stepped on to the leaf-strewn edge of Redemption River Bridge. A breeze sang through the green leaves and whispered around him, tickling like small fingers and bringing the wet scent of the red, muddy river to his nostrils.

Muscles stiff from long hours of riding, Sloan stretched in the May sunlight and listened to the crackle of his neck as he looked around. The river narrowed here, near the ancient bridge, then widened on its restless journey toward the town of Redemption. A knot had formed in his gut the moment the river had come into view. *Redemption* was a misnomer if he ever heard one. *Condemnation* was a better term.

Beneath the picturesque bridge, water trickled and gurgled, peaceful this time of year but still corroding the rocks and earth, eating away its foundation—a fitting metaphor for his hometown.

Sloan had never expected to cast another shadow in Redemption, Oklahoma, or to breathe the same air as Police

Chief Dooley Crawford—or his daughter, Annie. A dozen years later, here he was.

"Never say never," he muttered through three days' growth of whiskers. Traveling cross-country on a motorcycle with nothing but a duffel bag didn't afford luxury. Not that he couldn't have them if he wanted, but the good citizens of Redemption didn't need that information. They believed the worst of their "bad seed" and he hadn't come back to change their minds.

Only one person and one scenario could have coaxed him back to the place that had both destroyed and made him. Lydia. And she was dying.

The pain of that knowledge was a hot boulder in his belly, a fist around his heart tight enough to choke him to his knees. Sometimes life stunk.

He cast a hard-eyed squint across the riverbank toward the historic little town that despised him. They called him trouble. Like father, like son. With a throaty, humorless laugh, Sloan climbed back on the seat and kick-started the bike.

"Prepare yourself, Redemption, because trouble's back in town."

G.I. Jack spotted him first. The grizzled-gray Dumpster diver had just crawled out of the industrial-size receptacle behind Bracketts' furniture store when he heard the rumble. Any man with salt in his blood recognized the sweet music of a Harley-Davidson motorcycle. Though G.I. Jack couldn't recognize the model, he recognized the rider.

He rapped the side of the trash bin with his knuckles and hollered, "Popbottle, get out here this minute. You ain't gonna believe your eyes."

Popbottle Jones—so named because of an unfortunate length of cervical vertebrae—rose from the proverbial ashes of someone else's junk and snapped off his miner's lamp.

"Pray tell, G.I., what are you prattling on about?"

"Sloan Hawkins is back in town, bigger than life and scarier-looking than old Slewfoot himself, riding like some dark knight on a Harley."

Despite his advanced age, Popbottle Jones scrambled up from the Dumpster, hopped with practiced agility to the paved alley, and hurried to the end of the building for a better view. To the surprise of neither man, others had also spotted the unlikely visitor.

Tooney Deer stood at the yawning bay entrance of Tooney's Tune-Up, wiping his hands on a red mechanic's rag. Eighty-something handywoman Ida June Click paused in hammering a new awning over Redemption Register and yelled down at Kitty Wainright and Cheyenne Rhodes, who were just arriving at the newspaper office with a notice about the new women's shelter.

Across the street, Roberta Prine scurried out of the Curl Up and Dye Beauty Salon, mouth hanging open in both shock and thrill. Strips of shiny foil poked from her head like antennae, as if she was waiting to be beamed aboard the mother ship. She fished in her pocket for her cell phone. This was news. Big news.

Miriam Martinelli was spritzing Windex on the plate glass of the Sugar Shack Bakery in a never-ending battle against dust and fingerprints. Her employee, Sassy Carlson, pointed a roll of paper towels at the passerby.

"Who is *that?*"

"Well, I declare." Miriam plunked the Windex bottle on a round table and shaded her eyes with a large, bony hand. The dark rider roared past. "It's him, come back. And not a moment too soon. Praise be to Jesus."

"Who, Miriam? Who is it?"

Miriam cast a look over her shoulder, and sure enough,

Police Chief Dooley Crawford had wrenched back in his chair and was coming over, leaving his coffee and cinnamon roll. If time hadn't faded the issue, he wasn't going to like what he was about to see. Nor would his daughter.

"What are you two gawking at?" the chief asked, patting his shirt pocket for the ever-present roll of antacids. "Santie Claus coming down Main Street in the middle of May?"

The Harley had reached the red light by now. The rider eased to a stop with one black-booted foot balancing the massive bike. A thick silver chain rode low on the heel of the boot, giving it a dangerous look—as if the rider himself didn't look dangerous enough.

Chief Dooley Crawford grunted once, shoved a Rolaids between his lips, and stormed out of the bakery.

Home-health nurse Annie Markham was in the rose-colored kitchen, one hand on the oak cabinet where she kept Lydia's medications, when she heard the back door open. She stilled, cocked her head to one side and listened.

Her patient, the elderly Miss Lydia, was lying down. Annie's two kids were at school. No one else was supposed to be in Lydia Hawkins's beautiful old Victorian.

Annie listened again to be certain the house wasn't settling and heard the creak of footsteps. A twinge of alarm tickled the hair on her arms. "Who in the world…"

No one locked doors in Redemption. Nothing bad had happened here for nearly thirty years. Not since Lydia's no-account brother, Clayton, killed a man over a gambling debt. This was a good town, a safe town.

"Who is it?" she called.

A man's voice came back, smooth and deep. "Lydia?"

Her anxiety evaporated. Someone had come to visit her sick patient. Probably Popbottle Jones. The odd old gentleman had been coming around more and more since Lydia's health had gotten so bad. Strange, though, that he would enter through the back way via the gardens instead of knocking on the front door. Stranger still, he hadn't knocked at all.

"I'll be right there," she said.

In case the visitor wasn't Mr. Jones, Annie grabbed the closest weapon, a saucepan, and started out of the kitchen.

One step into the living room and she froze again, pan held aloft.

A hulking shape stood in shadow just inside the French doors leading out to the garden veranda. This was not Pop-bottle Jones. This was a big, bulky, dangerous-looking man. She raised the pan higher.

"What do you want?"

"Annie?" He stepped into the light.

All the blood drained from Annie's head. Her mouth went dry as saltines. "Sloan Hawkins?"

The man removed a pair of silver aviator sunglasses and hung them on the neck of his black rock 'n' roll T-shirt. He'd rolled the sleeves up, baring muscular biceps. A pair of eyes too blue to define narrowed, looking her over as though he were a wolf and she a bunny rabbit.

Annie suppressed an annoying shiver.

It was Sloan all right, though older and with more muscle. His nearly black hair was shorter now—no more bad-boy curl over the forehead, but bad boy screamed off him in waves just the same. He was devastatingly handsome, in a tough, rugged, manly kind of way. The years had been kind to Sloan Hawkins.

She really wanted to hate him, but she'd already wasted too much emotion on this outlaw. With God's help she'd learned to forgive. But she wasn't about to forget.

Mouth twitching in a face that needed a shave, Sloan

stretched his arms out to the sides. "You can put away your weapon. I'm unarmed."

She glanced at the forgotten saucepan and then lowered it to her side. After what he'd done, she should thump him with it for good measure.

She found her voice. "The bad penny returns."

The quirk of humor evaporated. His expression went flat and hard. "That's what they say."

"Sneaking in the back way, too. Typical. Sneak in. Sneak out."

Annie didn't know why she'd said that. She wasn't normally hateful, but Sloan had walked out on her twelve years ago without a word. To say she was shocked at his sudden, unexpected reappearance would be a massive understatement. Shocked, yes, but deeper emotions rattled around in her belly and set her insides to trembling. Anxiety. Anger. Hurt. All of them were stupid because she'd been over Sloan and that difficult time for years.

"You Redemption folks sure know how to roll out the welcome mat," he said in a quiet voice edged with steel. He reached in the back pocket of his tattered jeans and pulled out a yellow paper. "No more than hit town and I get a ticket. Compliments of your old man. He still loves me, too."

She ignored the *too*. What had he expected after what he'd done? A brass band and helium balloons? "You must have broken the law."

Gaze holding hers, Sloan slid the ticket back into his pocket. "That's what he always thought. Why change now?"

She wasn't going to get into this. There had been a lifetime of animosity between Sloan and her police-chief father. Apparently, time didn't change some things. She had a little animosity going herself, come to think of it.

"I suppose you want to see your aunt." Though why he'd bothered to come now, when time was running out, mystified her. Where had he been all these years? If he cared anything for the elderly aunt who'd taken him in when no one else would, he should have come home before now.

"Brilliant deduction, Sherlock. Considering I just rode thirteen hundred miles and I'm in her house, I'd say you're right." He shifted his weight to one hip. Something metallic jingled at his feet.

"Still got a smart mouth, I see."

"One of my many talents." He allowed a small display of teeth that looked nothing like a smile. "What are you doing here? The welcome committee send you out to harass me?"

"You think too highly of yourself, Sloan. No one knew you were coming and I doubt anyone cares."

"Ouch." He crossed his arms over that muscled-up chest. "When did you grow fangs?"

Annie drew in a deep breath. She wasn't a rude person, but Sloan's sudden appearance seemed to bring out the worst in her. If she was any kind of Christian, she'd stop letting him affect her right now.

"I'm Lydia's nurse as well as her friend. I care for and about her." She said the last as a dig. So much for not letting him get under her skin. *She* cared about the elderly woman who was everyone's friend. *She* was here for Lydia. He hadn't been. But then, "that Hawkins boy" had a history of running from responsibility.

He frowned. "A nurse. Full-time?"

Apparently, he hadn't been in close contact or he would know his aunt was dying. "I look after her during the day. She stays alone at night, though she shouldn't. Her choice, though."

He swallowed. "How bad is she?"

Some of the fire went out of her.

"Some days are better than others," she said softly. "But her heart is failing fast. I'm sorry, Sloan." And she meant it.

With his hands fisted at his sides and a hard line to his mouth, he looked lethal. If sheer will could cure Lydia's heart disease, Sloan would make it happen.

"Why isn't she in the hospital?"

"Surely you know your aunt better than that. She wants to die here in her own home with her gardens and memories around her."

He swallowed again and she could see he hadn't been prepared for the news to be this bad.

"Her heart is only functioning at about twenty percent. She puts on a good show for company, but she tires easily."

Sloan had no flip response. Annie would have felt better if he had. With a short nod, he headed to the staircase and started up.

"Sloan."

He stopped, one hand on the polished banister as he looked down with narrowed eyes and a strange little twist to his mouth. "What now? You want to frisk me?"

The smart mouth was back. She was going to ignore it. "Lydia can't negotiate the stairs anymore. We moved her things to the garden room."

Those stunning eyes fell closed for three seconds before he retraced his steps and headed toward the opposite side of the house. But in those three seconds, she saw past Sloan's tough facade the way she had in high school. Whether from guilt or out of love for his aunt, he was hurting.

Annie didn't want to think of Sloan Hawkins as vulnerable or sensitive. She wanted to remember him as the self-centered teenager who'd abandoned her when she'd needed him most. Better yet, she wanted him to go back to wherever he'd been hiding and leave well enough alone.

As soon as he was out of sight, Annie slithered onto the couch and put her face in her hands.

The wild and troubled boy she'd loved in high school was back in Redemption messing with her emotions and threatening her hard-earned peace of mind.

Looking upward, she murmured a prayer. "Lord, I know Lydia needs him and I'm trying to be glad for her. But Sloan Hawkins can't possibly bring anything but trouble." She glanced toward the staircase. "Especially to me."

Chapter Two

You could have knocked him over with a feather. Or with a two-cup, stainless-steel saucepan. Sloan's lips quivered.

He'd expected to run into Annie Crawford sooner or later, but he hadn't been prepared to see her here in Lydia's house, working as a nurse.

His smile disappeared before it could bloom. She wasn't Annie Crawford anymore. She'd married Joey Markham, a decent-enough guy, had kids, made a life.

Good. Fantastic. No reason for him to go on feeling guilty about the way they'd parted.

He did anyway. Like his mother's disappearance, Annie was an issue he'd never fully resolved.

His whole body had gone into shock the minute she'd stepped out of the kitchen with that pot in her hands. He was furious about his reaction, but there it was. With her large green eyes and Cameron Diaz cheekbones, Annie had blossomed from a pretty girl into a stunner. Seeing her again had made him feel weak and needy.

He despised weakness, particularly in himself. Childhood

and the military had taught him that. Be strong. Be tough. Never let them see you sweat.

He wiped at the moisture on his forehead. Encountering Annie had made him sweat.

There'd been other women in his life, though none in a while. His business soaked up most of his time. But the girl he'd been crazy about as a teen had lingered in his mind. A turn of phrase, a song on the radio, a woman with high cheekbones could start the memories flowing fast and painful. He'd long ago boycotted Cameron Diaz movies.

He'd have to boycott Annie Crawford Markham, too, though it wouldn't be easy with her working here.

She was none too happy to see him, either, but she had good reason. What she didn't know was that his reasons for leaving town were every bit as good as her reasons to despise him. He hadn't told her then, and he sure wouldn't tell her now why he'd had to leave. She'd never done one thing to deserve the grief dealt to her. Nothing except love the son of Redemption's most reviled criminal.

He sighed and rubbed the bridge of his nose. Protection was his business. He'd loved Annie enough to protect her at eighteen. He'd protect her now with his silence.

Sloan's thoughts ping-ponged in a dozen directions as he traversed the long hallway toward his aunt's new living quarters. He hated knowing she couldn't climb the stairs anymore. Strong, independent Lydia would hate it even more, but unlike her ill-tempered nephew, she would put on a happy face and find a blessing in moving downstairs.

Sloan grunted. He saw no blessing in dying.

Even after all this time, his feet knew the way through the big Victorian that had been his only refuge as a child. The house was still stunning with its gleaming oak trim, sky-high ceilings, and huge windows for admiring the considerable view. The upstairs held four bedrooms and baths, two of which boasted sitting rooms with balconies and fire-places. He'd spent his teen years in one while Lydia had lived in the master suite overlooking the expansive backyard known as the wedding garden. Though surrounded by the Hawkins's wealth, Sloan had felt like an outcast tainted by his father's crime.

The vast downstairs was typical Victorian with an elegant parlor, a living room, the country kitchen and formal dining room complete with butler's pantry, a library and study along with the garden room—a sunny space surrounded by windows looking out upon the backyard and Lydia's beloved flower gardens.

It was to this room he came and found the oak-paneled door ajar.

His throat squeezed. Aunt Lydia lay on a hospital bed, her hands holding a book, a pale purple lap robe over her legs. She was dressed as he always thought of her in a print house dress; this one was blue. Oxygen hissed from a bedside tank into a tube looped around her head. Even from this distance he could see how frail she was.

She couldn't be dying. Times like this he wished he believed in prayer the way she did.

He rapped a knuckle on the open door and said, "Aunt Lydia?"

Her head swiveled toward him. She released the book—a worn black Bible—and reached out, smiling wide. The joy in her face filled him with hope that he was more than Redemption gave him credit for.

"Sloan. You've come home."

Sloan went to her then and took the outstretched fingers. They were cold. He kissed her cheek, breathed in her talcum-powder scent.

"Heard my best girl wasn't feeling so hot."

"Who told?" Her eyes were a tad too bright, her cheeks a little too rosy.

"You did." Although the phone call from Ulysses E. Jones had gotten him moving.

"When?" she asked, disbelieving.

Still holding her pale, slender hand, he slid onto the chair next to her bed. "When you refused to go to Egypt with me."

"I always wanted to see the pyramids." The wheeze in her chest made him want to kick something.

"We'll reschedule as soon as you're feeling better."

She patted his hand but didn't say anything. The silence tore at him, a truth too terrible to be voiced.

"We're only on trip number seven, Auntie. You can't quit on me now."

Her eyes sparkled. "You and your lists."

Sloan didn't remind her that the trip list was her doing. After his business had begun to prosper, he'd asked her to write down ten places she'd like to visit. He'd taken her to seven of them and had a dozen more in mind. If he could give her the world, he would.

The oxygen hiss reminded him that time was running out to give her anything but himself.

"Fancy necklace you're wearing there, Miss Lydia."

She patted the green oxygen tubing. "You know me. I like to look pretty. Did you talk to Annie?"

"You could have warned me."

"Didn't know you were coming."

She wouldn't have told him anyway. After Annie had married, Sloan refused to discuss her. What was the point? If Lydia hadn't shoved the information on him, he wouldn't have known about her kids.

"She's divorced now."

He jerked. He'd missed that piece of information. "Too bad."

"Yes, it is. Annie's a good Christian girl and a great friend to me. Joey didn't do right by her."

Sloan felt his jaw tighten. "What do you mean?"

And when did Annie get religion?

"There was gossip about Joey and other women for a long time." Lydia paused for a breath. Her chest heaved. "Two years ago, he left Annie for a woman over in Iron Post. He doesn't even bother to visit those kids."

Anger stirred in Sloan's belly. If he had Joey Markham's pretty-boy face in sight, he'd break his nose. "She chose him."

"After you left."

"That was a long time ago. We were kids. We both got over it and moved on."

Lydia studied him for an extended second. She was wearing down fast, a fact that made him ache.

"Be nice, Sloan. Annie's had enough heartache."

Go ahead and lay on the guilt. He was used to it. "Why, Aunt Lydia, I'm always a nice guy."

He showed his teeth and she swatted his arm the way she'd done when he was a kid. "Are you hungry?"

This time the smile was real. Aunt Lydia was a true Southern lady who believed in the power of food. "I'll grab something later."

"There's plenty in the kitchen. Annie makes enough to feed the Seventh Cavalry. Meals are not part of her job, but I can't make her stop."

He'd scrounge the kitchen after Annie went home. "Nice of her. I'm here now. I'll cook for both of us."

"You and Annie can work that out."

He didn't think so.

"I don't think Annie likes having me around that much." But she'd have to deal with him anyway. Lydia was his aunt and he wasn't budging.

"That's because you look like something the cat dragged in," she said with affection. "What did you do, hitchhike?"

He glanced down at his tattered jeans and scuffed boots. He probably smelled a little ripe, too. "Motorcycle."

"Can't afford an airplane?"

He grinned. She knew better. Lately, he'd considered buying one of his own. "I had some serious thinking to do."

"Did you get it done?"

He managed a short laugh. "No."

"Then you shouldn't be sitting here—" she paused to take a breath "—with a wheezy old lady. Go on back to Virginia and save the world. Your work is too important to be worrying over me."

"You're not going to run me off that easy." As long as he had his smart phone and a fax machine, he could work from anywhere. "I'm staying as long as you need me."

"Are you sure about that, honey? You were always so adamant about never coming back to Redemption. I don't want you hurt again."

Which meant the dirty laundry in a small town wasn't forgotten, no matter how long a man stayed away. "I want to be wherever you are. That's all that matters."

"Then give me a kiss and go take a shower."

She was tiring. He could hear fatigue in the staccato speech and see the tinge of gray around her lips. Even a short conversation was too much for her fragile heart.

Obediently, he kissed her crepe-paper cheek, his insides crying like a baby, and headed for his old upstairs bedroom and a long, hot shower.

As he grabbed the banister and started up the curvy wooden staircase, he heard Annie's voice in the kitchen. Without guilt, he stopped to listen. He'd discovered the value of eavesdropping, whether with a planted listening device or an ordinary ear.

"Oh, not again." She sounded none too happy. "I am terribly sorry, Mr. Granger. Okay, I will. Yes, right away."

Then the receiver thumped hard on to the cradle. A whimper of dismay was followed by the scrape of chair legs and another whimper.

Sloan frowned and stepped around the wall into the warm, sunny kitchen.

Annie sat at the round table, head down on folded arms. Honey-blond hair spilled over a long barrette onto the polished oak. Her shoulders heaved.

Oh, man. Was she crying?

In answer, Annie drew in a hiccoughing breath and sniffed.

"Hey, hey," he said softly, out of his element and unsure of what to do at this point. Give him a terrorist or a man with a gun any day. A crying woman was far more frightening.

He reached out, hand hovering above the soft-looking hair. *Don't do it. Don't touch her.*

She sniffed again.

He touched her.

Someone was touching her.

Annie sat upright. Sloan hovered next to her chair…and his hand was on her hair.

Heart thudding erratically, she jerked away.

Sloan's hand was left suspended in midair. He folded it against his side.

"What are you doing?" she asked. And why did she sound breathless?

"Listening to you cry. What's wrong?" Forehead wrinkled, mouth tight, he looked as if he wanted to strangle someone.

Hopefully not her. On second thought, after the phone call, she might let him.

"Nothing."

"Oh right, sure. Peeling onions again."

In spite of herself, Annie nearly smiled. "You were always such an idiot."

"Another of my talents." He handed her a napkin from the hand-painted napkin holder Lydia had bought on a trip to Japan.

Hoping to regain her composure, Annie took her time, dabbed at each corner of her eyes, dotted underneath, then patted her cheekbones.

Sloan turned a chair around backward and straddled it. "Tell me."

"I haven't talked to you in twelve years. Why start now?" She sounded as petulant as she felt.

"Explain why you're crying and I'll go away."

She rolled her eyes. "For another twelve years?"

His expression was bland, but something flickered in those electric-blue eyes. "You're stuck with me for a while."

Annie's stomach dipped. Sloan Hawkins underfoot day after day? "You're not serious."

"I am." He studied the end of his fingernail. "Who was that on the phone?"

Her mouth dropped open. She couldn't believe this man. Less than an hour in town and he was prying into her life? "Were you eavesdropping?"

He abandoned the troublesome nail to lift both palms. "Well, yeah. So tell me unless you want a bug on the phone."

"A what?"

He didn't seem too happy about the strange statement, and now Annie was the one who wanted to pry. What had Sloan been doing since high school?

"I'm being an idiot again," he said. "You need an aspirin or something?"

"No, I need for my son to behave himself." Tears pushed up behind her nose. She was sure her eyes had gone all watery. "He's in trouble at school. Again."

"And? What did he do?"

She couldn't believe this. She hadn't communicated with Sloan Hawkins since before her senior prom and now he was sitting across the table expecting her to spill out her troubles the way she used to.

Oh, why not? No one else was listening and no matter what he said, Sloan would be gone before the week was out. He owed her a little child-rearing advice.

"Justin got in a fight."

"Is he okay?"

She hadn't expected him to show concern. "He won't be when I get through with him."

Sloan whistled softly. "Mean Mama. Boys fight. It's normal."

"Not at school." Besides, what would Sloan know about normal? "He never behaved this way until—" She pushed up from the table. She was not going to talk about Joey or the divorce. Not to Sloan Hawkins. "Tell Lydia I'll be back in time to give her her medications."

Sloan unwound his tall body from the wooden chair. "Need company?"

Right. Like she wanted any more problems in her life. Without answering, she grabbed her purse and hurried out the door.

She was back in thirty minutes, flustered, clearly upset, and dragging a belligerent-faced boy who looked like a miniature, male version of his mother.

Kicked back on the flowered sofa, answering e-mails on

his smart phone, Sloan pretended to ignore their tense conversation.

"There are three days left until school is out," Annie was saying. "Why did you have to get in a fight now?"

"He was picking on me."

"What did he do?"

The kid clammed up.

Annie's hair had come loose from the big barrette and lay on her shoulders. She shoved angrily at an unlucky strand.

"If you won't tell me what happened, then I have to assume you did something you shouldn't have."

The conversation was giving Sloan a serious case of déjà vu. He shifted, uncomfortable.

The boy—Justin, wasn't it?—crossed his arms and glared at the wall behind Annie. Whatever had happened, he wasn't going to tell his mother. And that had Sloan wondering.

"To hear your side of the story—" Annie said. She had her hands on her hips, ready to tear into the boy. "—it's never your fault and everyone picks on you."

This wasn't his business. He should keep his mouth shut. Exhaling a single huff of air, Sloan lowered his feet to the floor and leaned forward. He'd always been lousy at remaining neutral. "Maybe they do."

Annie whirled on him, green eyes shooting sparks. "Are you still here?"

She was gorgeous all fired up.

He shrugged. "I'm a male. We like to watch explosions."

Justin snickered. Annie glowered. "Stay out of this."

Sloan lifted both hands in surrender. Annie was not in the mood for his jokes.

She poked a finger in the boy's face. "You'd better start talking, Justin."

"Or what, Mom? You gonna ground me again?" Justin made a rude noise. "Like I care. Big whoopin' deal."

Sorry kid, you went too far. Sloan shoved against his knees and stood, rising to his full six feet two. He kept his tone mild but firm. "Don't smart-mouth your mother."

A little squeak escaped Annie. Her mouth opened and closed.

Lip curled, Justin glared at him. "Who are *you?*"

Sloan offered a hand as if the two had been introduced at church. "Sloan Hawkins. Miss Lydia is my aunt."

Justin stared at the hand for two beats and then shook. The kid had a wimpy handshake. *Better toughen up, kid. Life is hard.*

"You owe your mother an apology."

"What do you know about it?" But Justin dropped his gaze, some of his belligerence fading.

"I know she's a good mother who went running when you needed her. Better appreciate having someone in your corner." This time Annie didn't tell him to back off. A good thing because he wouldn't anyway. No one was talking to Annie like that in his presence. Not even her son.

Justin studied the tops of his untied sneakers and mumbled in a more polite tone. "Am I grounded?"

Annie pushed. "Are you going to tell me why you hit Ronnie Prine?"

"No. But he deserved it."

Sloan was starting to believe the kid. He'd been there, done that. Bullies didn't change. If they found a tender spot, they'd pick at it until you bled or exploded. Justin had exploded.

Annie sighed, a long-suffering huff of air. "You have in-school suspension for the rest of the week. I suppose that's enough, *if* you promise to control your temper and stay out of trouble." Tiredly, she rubbed two fingers over her forehead. "Now go finish your homework."

The kid pivoted to leave the room. Sloan stopped him. "Wait a minute."

Eyes rolling, body cocked to one side in an expression of annoyance, Justin said, "What?"

"Don't you have something to say to your mother?"

Justin squirmed, clearly not wanting to lose face, but when neither adult relented, he muttered, "Sorry, Mom."

Sloan narrowed his eyes and studied the lanky boy. Something about his stance was uncannily familiar. "How old are you, kid?"

Annie shot him a long look.

"Eleven. What's it to you?"

Maybe more than either of us knows.

Eleven. Justin was eleven. With that worrisome little tidbit eating into his brain like a woodworm, Sloan did the math and considered the possibilities.

Nah, he couldn't be.

Could he?

Chapter Three

Bluetooth headset attached to his ear like an oversize cockroach, Sloan exited his bedroom with an armload of clothes to toss in the washer.

"Yeah, send Blake and Griffith with the ambassador's family. Some segments of Manila aren't excited about his mission. We may encounter problems there. Tell the team to be on their toes." As head of Worldwide Security Solutions, he contracted with the government and military on a regular basis. This latest assignment in the Philippines had him worried. Muslim extremists had infiltrated the area. "Sure, no problem. How's the issue in Afghanistan we discussed yesterday?"

Listening intently, he rounded the top of the stairs…and slammed into Annie. The bundle of clothes went flying. Annie stumbled back and started to fall. Instinctively, Sloan reached out, grasped her upper arms and yanked forward. Annie ended up cradled in his arms, against his chest.

His first sensation, besides the adrenaline pumping like pistons through his bloodstream, was the smell of her hair. He'd teased her in high school about washing her hair in apple juice. Apparently, she still did.

The second thought was of how she fit against him, curved in all the right places and softer than silk. She must have been stunned, too, because she didn't move for several seconds. Several torturous seconds while he flashed back to age nineteen and the wild, desperate love he'd felt for Annie Crawford.

His throat went dry. This was not good, not good at all.

He told his arms to release her. He told his legs to step back one stair step. His well-trained body, capable of taking out an enemy in three-point-six seconds, would not obey.

The voice in his ear said his name. Once. Twice.

"Later," he muttered, too distracted to remember the business conversation.

While he battled inwardly, both reveling in the touch and dismayed at the yearning, Annie stiffened.

"Excuse me," she said, voice muffled against his Harley T-shirt. When he didn't move, she wiggled away, retreating one step so that he was looking down into her upturned face.

She wasn't happy about the unexpected contact either. Above the blush cresting on her cheekbones, her big green eyes looked even bigger. Her chest rose and fell like an escapee, and her mouth was pinched tight and tilted down. She looked repulsed.

His touch repulsed her.

Grinding his molars, Sloan gave a short nod he hoped passed for an apology and bent to retrieve his laundry. Silently, Annie gathered a shirt and a pair of jeans from the banister. As Sloan reached for the items, she held one end and he the other. Their eyes met and held, as well. A feeling rose between them that he did not want to identify. A feeling more dangerous and disturbing to his peace of mind than the work in Afghanistan.

Finally, he grumbled, "Thanks," and bounded down the stairs like a man running from his past.

* * *

Sloan and Annie tiptoed around each other for another three days before the ice began to thaw. He didn't know why that mattered except being in the same house all day with a silent frozen woman was pure discomfort.

He was plagued by memories of the way they'd been in high school, made worse by that moment on the stairs.

The day after school dismissed, Annie brought both her kids to the house because of sitter problems.

"Never mind about your work rules," his aunt had said to Annie. "This is my house and if I want to invite those children, I will. Tell your boss I said so."

It was not yet seven o'clock when they arrived, and Sloan sat at the kitchen table, draped over a copy of *USA TODAY* and a fragrant cup of extra-sweet coffee.

"Morning," he mumbled, determined to be civil. "I made coffee."

"Thank you." If she got any stiffer, she'd be cardboard.

Justin slouched in, all arms and legs and loose ends, looking like trouble but saying nothing. The kid had an attitude as bad as Sloan's.

Sloan studied the kid with interest. After fiddling with the dates until he had brain lock, he had concluded that Justin was not his son. Annie had married the summer after Sloan's departure—which allowed time for Joey to be Justin's father. Sloan considered asking Annie straight out, but figured he was wrong anyway, and she already thought he was pond scum. The boy looked nothing like him. Their only similarity was a bad attitude which Sloan was fairly certain was not genetic. No use starting trouble. He had enough of that without trying.

Last night, he'd ridden his motorcycle into town to pick up Lydia's prescriptions and could feel the stares burning a hole in his back. He'd no more than given the Hawkins name to the pharmacist when a woman approached him. Sloan hackled. His memories of Roberta Prine were not fond ones.

"Say, you're Sloan Hawkins, aren't you? Clayton Hawkins's son." She'd snapped her fingers as if trying to remember something. "And his wife—what was her name? Worked over at the diner? Janie?"

Sloan skewered her with a dark glance. If she was trying to get a rise out of him by pretending ignorance, she was succeeding.

"Joni," he muttered through clenched teeth.

"That's right. Now I remember." Right. As if she'd actually forgotten. "She's the one that run off with a trucker, wasn't she? Sure was a crazy thing to do, leaving you behind and all. Did you ever hear from her again?"

Never let 'em see you sweat.

With a cocky grin he didn't feel, Sloan leaned in and imitated her tone. "Say, aren't you the mom of that mean little creep, Ronnie? And isn't that your broom parked by the curb outside?"

Roberta jerked back, face flushing bright red. "Well, I never!"

Sloan showed his teeth in a feral smile. "Now you have."

Taking the white sack from the stunned pharmacist, Sloan spun on his boot heels. A titter of conversation followed him.

"That's the thanks I get for being neighborly."

"Never was much good."

Sloan had clenched his fists and kept moving, exactly as he'd learned to do as a boy.

Well, he wasn't a boy anymore. He would handle the Redemption gossip for Lydia's sake. What he wasn't handling particularly well was the tension between him and Annie.

Lifting his coffee cup, he watched her move around the kitchen to prepare Lydia's breakfast. If any woman could look good in nurse's scrubs, Annie did. This morning her hair was on her shoulders, held back from her forehead by a brown clip of some kind. Wispy little curls flirted around her cheekbones.

Ah, those cheekbones. He remembered the feel of her silky skin beneath his thumbs, the salty taste of her tears when he'd butted heads with her father.

Sloan slid his gaze away from Annie and the torrent of reminders. Why couldn't he get his brain under control?

Justin slouched into the room across from Sloan. His dark blond hair was still damp, as if his mother had forced him to water it down. Sloan had done the same thing when he was a kid. Splash with water, hit it once with a comb and call it done. The teenage years and girls would change Justin's grooming habits.

"Morning," Sloan said.

Justin gave him one of those looks that said he'd rather die than be awake this early. Sloan grinned against his coffee cup.

Annie walked by and stroked a hand lovingly over the boy's messy hair.

That quick, Sloan was tossed back a dozen years. He had been hanging out at the river with a bunch of other kids. Some guy had called him the son of a slut and a jailbird. Naturally, he'd punched the goon in the face. This hadn't gone over well with the goon's friends and before he could make an escape, Sloan had six guys kicking his ribs in. Annie had come flying to his defense, screaming her head off that she was going to tell her father on them. They'd backed off, and she'd knelt beside him on the ground, cradled his head and stroked his hair.

That was the day he'd fallen in love with Annie.

He closed his eyes against the memory, and when he opened them again, a dimpled darling with big brown eyes, a hot pink headband, and a nearly white ponytail stood at his side.

"You're Sloan. Justin told me about you." She frowned up at him with interest. "You don't look that mean."

A pitcher of juice in one hand and a glass in the other, Annie looked aghast. "Delaney!"

Sloan chuckled, glad for the distraction. His head was giving him fits. "I'm never mean to little girls with ponytails."

She climbed up on the chair beside him. Her swaying ponytail brushed his arm. "I drew you a picture."

"Yeah?" He knew next to nothing about kids, but this one charmed him.

She displayed a neatly colored, crudely drawn playground, complete with the smiley-faced sun. "You can hang it on the refrigerator. That's what Mom does. Have you got any Scotch tape? I'll hang it for you."

"Why don't you show your drawing to Miss Lydia first?" Annie said. "Ask her if she feels up to coming to the table this morning."

More and more of Lydia's time was spent inside the garden room.

"Okay." Delaney hopped down and bounced out of the kitchen, taking a ray of sunshine with her.

"Cute kid." he said. "How old is she?"

"Nine." Annie's whole face softened with love. "Delaney is a blessing, has been from the moment she was born."

Unlike the churlish boy? he wanted to ask, but didn't. Justin was sitting right across the table, wolfing down half a box of Cheerios.

Almost immediately, Delaney skipped back into the kitchen and opened the refrigerator. "Miss Lydia liked my picture."

"I knew she would. Is she up to sitting with us for breakfast?"

"Not this morning, she said. Maybe tomorrow."

Annie and Sloan exchanged unhappy glances.

"That's what I figured, but I wanted to ask." She slid Lydia's breakfast plate onto a tray, added a tiny cup of pills and started toward the doorway.

"I'll take that," Sloan said and swallowed the last of his coffee. The fresh-ground brew went down smooth and warm.

"Thanks." She smiled. And that simple little action made his belly flip-flop. He wanted to blame the caffeine, but he was a realist. Annie was getting to him big time.

He reached for the tray. Their hands touched. He grunted and made his escape.

Frankly, after a week he needed something better to do than to stare at Annie and relive memories of a painful past. A man of action, he was accustomed to fourteen-hour days and frequent trips all over the globe. Here in Redemption his smart phone kept him busy but not busy enough to keep his eyes and mind off Annie. Not being a man who particularly enjoyed suffering, he didn't want to notice her. She obviously didn't want to be around him, either.

He spent as much time with Lydia as her health allowed, but his sick aunt slept more than she was awake. When she felt up to it, he carried her to the veranda for some fresh air. Yesterday, he'd found the weed-whacker and gone to work on the fast-growing weeds around the porches. Today he'd find a lawnmower if he had to buy a new one. Anything to stay clear of Annie and those troubling memories.

Annie watched Sloan all the way down the hallway, walking in a loose-limbed strut exactly like Justin's. She'd been terrified when he'd roared in on his Harley and intruded on her safe world. People in town were already talking, speculating on where he'd been and what he'd been doing. Most remembered him with sympathy as that poor little Hawkins boy whose mother ran off and whose father died in prison. But not everyone had been as kind. Some said he was a drug dealer. She'd done her best to squelch that rumor. Not that she had a clue what his life was like, but the Sloan she remembered was scared of anything addictive. He'd said his life was out of control enough. He wasn't about to let drugs take over.

"Mom, can I go to Brett's and play video games?"

She turned to find her son at her elbow. "Maybe later. I'll have to call his mother."

Justin's gaze followed Sloan down the hallway. "You like that guy?"

The question came out of nowhere. Annie turned to study her son's expression. "I don't even know him."

"That's not what Ronnie says."

Ah. So that was it. She should have known someone like Roberta Prine would resurrect the past relationship between her and Sloan. "What exactly did he say to you?"

"Nothing. Just stuff. He's a loser."

"Was that why the two of you got in a fight?"

Avoiding her eyes, he hitched a shoulder. "Maybe."

Lord, forgive me for not believing in him.

She hooked an elbow around his neck and bumped his head with hers. He was nearly as tall as her now. By summer's end, he would likely surpass her. Someday he'd be as tall as his father.

"Rumors hurt people, Justin. You have to learn to ignore them. Okay?"

One bony shoulder hitched. "I guess."

Being a single mother was the most difficult job she'd ever tried to do. Justin had never been an easy child, but pre-adolescence was doing a number on him—and her.

"Mom?" He stared at his sneakers. The strings were untied, but she knew better than to get into an argument over that. She was learning to choose her battles.

"What, son?"

He fidgeted another moment. "I love you."

Annie's throat thickened with emotion. "Oh, baby, I love you, too. You're my heart, my life."

She kissed his cheek, something he rarely allowed these days and was gratified when he grinned and didn't yank away.

Delaney bounced into the room, her usual sunshiny self, with the handheld video game she'd gotten last Christmas. "Justin, will you play Pretty Miss Dress-Up with me?"

Annie could see how much her son did *not* want to play the girly game, but he stepped away from her and said, "Sure."

From the time Delaney had been born, Justin had doted on his baby sister. Regardless of his attitude in other areas, he was a gentle, loving brother. The knowledge gave her hope that beneath the sometimes sullen boy was a good man waiting to bloom. At least, that was what she prayed for.

She left her children side by side on the couch, heads bent over the electronic game, and headed to Lydia's room to begin their morning routine. When she reached the doorway, Sloan was standing next to the bed, his side angled away from Annie so he didn't know she was watching him. Lydia was propped up on a mile-high stack of pillows with the hospital table alongside, her oxygen cannula making its monotone hiss. Sloan's big, manly hands held a hairbrush which he was gently drawing through Lydia's white hair, over and over again.

Annie's chest constricted.

She didn't want to think of Sloan as tender. She wanted to think of him as a user, a troublemaker, a jerk of the highest magnitude.

But he wasn't always, a voice whispered.

She batted away the thought like a pesky fly and hurried back to the kitchen.

Company arrived at ten.

Sloan was behind the push-style lawnmower, sweating buckets, his T-shirt soaked when Annie stepped outside and asked him to help Lydia to the veranda.

"She prefers you to the wheelchair." Annie seemed irked to involve him, as if she could have done the job just fine alone. She likely could have.

Wiping sweat, he went into the kitchen, stuck his over-heated head under the faucet for a long, refreshing minute. When he came up, water sluicing, Annie stood next to him, a towel in hand. "Don't drip everywhere."

She sounded like a mother. Or a wife.

He clenched his teeth. Why did she have to be underfoot every day? Why couldn't someone besides Annie serve as Lydia's nurse? He would have taken a room at Redemption Motel, but what good was coming home if he didn't spend every spare moment with Lydia?

With an annoyed grunt, he grabbed the towel and scrubbed his face and head with more vigor than was needed, then went to do his aunt's bidding. With Annie handling the portable oxygen bottle, Sloan scooped Lydia into his arms. She felt frail and fragile, skin over bones, and Sloan's chest ached with sorrow. Before his very eyes, his aunt was fading away.

Out on the long, shady porch, Sloan encountered the man who'd telephoned him two weeks ago with the news that Lydia was unwell. Over the phone, Ulysses Jones sounded educated and well-to-do, but as Sloan recollected, Popbottle Jones didn't look a thing like his voice.

"Sit with us, Mr. Hawkins. I doubt you remember me, but I recall your mother very well."

Sloan stiffened. Lots of men had known his mother. "Yes, I remember you."

Who could forget the local Dumpster divers, Popbottle Jones and his quirky partner, G.I. Jack? They were notorious for their "recycling business" as well as for knowing pretty much everything in town.

"Your mother was a kind and generous heart."

Sloan relaxed onto a metal chair opposite his aunt, pathetically grateful to hear the compliment. "Yes, she was."

His mother had been a soft touch for anyone down on his luck or needing a place to crash for the night. After she'd left, Redemption seemed to have forgotten her good qualities. Sloan never had, though he'd been scared and angered by her abandonment. Sometimes he still couldn't believe she had driven away and left him.

Annie came through the French doors carrying a tray of lemonade. She slid the flowered tray onto the round patio table. Fresh lemons bobbed in a clear pitcher. "Lydia's recipe, though not as good as hers, I'm sure."

Lydia's lemonade was legend, as were the garden parties and weddings held here in the garden where lemonade had been the drink of choice.

"Are you okay out here?" Annie said to Lydia. "Do you need anything?"

"I'm fine, honey. Why don't you sit and visit a spell? You work too hard."

"I shouldn't." Annie glanced at Sloan and he had a feeling that her refusal had more to do with him than work.

"Sit down, Annie." The command came out much gruffer than he'd intended. But she sat.

Sloan didn't miss the glance Lydia and Popbottle Jones exchanged. He glowered at both of them.

"The mimosa is blooming," Lydia said, probably to break the tense silence.

Early summer was upon them, warm and shining. Pink mimosa blossoms cast a sweet perfume over the vast yard. Hummingbirds and bees competed for the sweet nectar, creating a constant, pleasant buzz. Most summers the garden—locally known as the Wedding Garden—was also abuzz with wedding preparations. Dozens of Redemption citizens had married in the Hawkins's backyard.

As if she couldn't sit still more than two minutes, Annie got up and busied herself with handing around glasses of lemonade. Dry from yard work, Sloan downed his in two drinks. The tart cold cut through the dust and thirst.

"Your roses look puny, Aunt Lydia." Ice rattled as he aimed his drippy glass toward a trellis covered in withered vines and limp pink flowers.

"They need tending, but…" Expression sad, Lydia lifted a hand tiredly. She, who had spent hours and hours tending and coddling this garden for her pleasure and the pleasure of others, had no more gardening left in her.

Now, as he took the time to really observe, Sloan saw the neglect taking a toll. More than the roses suffered. Weeds had taken over, choking out the young plants and hiding the old ones. Trees and bushes were overgrown and shaggy with more than a few dead branches. No bride had planned a wedding here in a long time.

Not that he cared about that, but Lydia would. Her beloved garden spread for more than an acre beyond the porch. A place of light and shade and peace, the garden had been here since the first Hawkins bride moved in after the Land Run of 1889. Occupants through the years had added their touches, and the garden had become a source of pride and pleasure to Aunt Lydia and the whole of Redemption.

"I recall some merry occasions in this garden," Popbottle Jones intoned.

"Me, too," Annie said. She'd perched again, close enough that Sloan smelled apples and had to fight down a miserable yearning. "I caught Claire Watson's bouquet right over there." She lifted one finger from her half-empty glass to point.

Sloan's chest tightened. He remembered that afternoon. Annie was a bridesmaid in pink, a hundred times more beautiful than the bride. A giggling batch of females had scrambled for the tossed bouquet, but as if guided by a homing device, the flowers had fallen into Annie's hands. Everyone in attendance had turned to look at him. Cat-calling male attendees had pounded him on the back and made remarks about the old ball and chain. Annie had blushed and looked so happy Sloan had wanted to marry her then and there.

He clunked the glass on the table. Ice cubes rattled. "I'll tend them." The words came out gruff, angry. Well, what if they had? He *was* angry, though mostly at himself.

When the gathered company gazed at him with surprised faces, he turned and left the porch.

Redemption's Plant Farm and Garden Center smelled green and wet. Customers browsed up and down the long aisles filled with flats and potted plants, some in flower, some not. A man in coveralls carried a burlap-wrapped tree in each hand while the woman with him rattled on about a bird bath and wind chimes. Outside workers loaded a truck with patio urns and garden furniture.

Sloan fisted his hands on his hips and gazed around at the bewildering array of plants, bags, sprays, and tools. He didn't know a lot about gardening but he wasn't about to let that stop him. In fact, he'd do more than water and feed the roses. He was dying for some sweaty, hard work to keep him busy. Mowing the lawn was quick. Revitalizing the garden his aunt loved would not be.

"May I help you, sir?" A familiar-looking woman in no-nonsense work pants and long-sleeved shirt approached him. Middle-aged, maybe older, she had short blond curls, a serious overbite and a healthy tan. Miller. Her name was Miller—

Delores, he thought—and her family had operated the plant farm for years.

"I want to revitalize my aunt's flower gardens. Any advice?"

"Depends on what you want to do. Who's your aunt? Maybe I know her tastes."

"Lydia Hawkins." He tensed, waiting for the relationship to register and the expected censure.

Recognition flickered but her expression remained mild, not the cold-faced glare he'd gotten at the drug store.

"Lydia. God love her. How is she doing?"

"Not well, but thanks for asking."

"I heard you'd come back. Figured Lydia's health had taken a turn." Frowning, she reached down and plucked a yellowed leaf from a flat of petunias. He was sure they were petunias because the little white plastic stick said so. "Best gardener in the county. I never knew how she managed the Wedding Garden on her own."

Sloan had helped some as a boy, though not nearly enough now that he looked back. He'd been good for little except causing trouble.

"She can't take care of them anymore. From the looks of things, she hasn't done much in years."

"I'd say you're right. I haven't seen her in here in a long time. Doesn't even get out to church that often and you know how faithful she is to the Lord."

More faithful than the Lord was to her, apparently.

"Can you help me out with the garden?" he asked. "Give me some idea of what I need and where to begin?"

"You planning to have weddings there again?"

The idea took him aback. "Hadn't thought about it."

"You should. Come on. Let's see what we can find."

She led the way to a counter strewn with papers, a trowel, a box of seed packets, a hunk of burlap and a good amount of loose, black dirt. She went behind the counter and bent down, disappearing from sight. Her muffled voice rose up to where he waited.

"This town needs that wedding garden. Tradition, you know. History matters here in Redemption. I suspect Lydia, bless her heart, needs it, too. You're a good nephew to do this."

Sloan's mouth quivered. First time he'd been accused of that.

"Somewhere in this mess I actually have files of my best customers. Sometimes even a photo or two. Customers like to brag on their handiwork and I like to see where my plants thrive. You can be sure I have plenty of Lydia's yard. Ah, here we go."

She popped up with a plain manila file boldly labeled "Lydia Hawkins." Inside was a mishmash of invoices and hand-written notes.

"See this picture?" She plopped a snapshot in front of him. "We can start with this."

"Okay." He still didn't know where to begin.

Mrs. Miller laughed. "I can see you're lost. Come on, then, I will load you up and give you a crash course. Then you call me or come by anytime you have a question. Got your truck?"

"Uh, no." He turned to glance out at the parking area. Two men were standing close to his bike, talking. His shoulders tensed. "I'm on my motorcycle."

"You can't carry supplies on a motorcycle. One of the boys can deliver. Let's get started." She hollered toward someone in the back. "Mack, bring a dolly. We got a live one."

She laughed again and Sloan decided he liked this no-nonsense woman. She didn't seem to care that he was the notorious Hawkins boy. He shot another look at the parking lot, found the men gone, and relaxed.

As Mrs. Miller dragged him from plants to fertilizers to animal repellents, she hollered out orders and greetings, stopping now and then to chat with customers.

Three people stopped Sloan to ask about Lydia, but other than a couple of curious stares and the men coveting his Harley, the outing was amazingly benign.

Would wonders never cease?

By the time he slipped on his shades and roared away on his bike, he'd bought several hundred dollars' worth of supplies and his head spun with advice. But a sense of excitement hummed in his veins. He didn't give a rip about pleasing the town, but he could restore the Wedding Garden for Lydia… and stay under Annie's radar at the same time.

As he approached the main section of town, he downshifted and cruised past stately homes, historic buildings and businesses that hadn't changed all that much in a decade.

For the first time since he'd returned, he really looked at the town he'd once called home. Redemption was a beautiful place, idyllic some would say, with neat green lawns and clean fresh air.

There was even a story that healing flowed in Redemption River—or some such nonsense as that.

Sloan gave a short, mirthless laugh.

It was a story, nothing more, meant to attract tourists.

According to his aunt and his mother, Redemption was a town of good and caring people. He'd spent his whole life wondering where they were.

Thinking about the river gave him the urge to ride out to the bridge. The gardening center wouldn't deliver until tomorrow anyway, and he sure wasn't doing anything else. The longer he could avoid Annie and the curious buzz she created in his veins, the better.

He circled around Town Square, catching a glimpse of Tooney Carter, who raised a hand in greeting. Sloan nodded. He and Tooney had fished together as boys and gotten into more than their share of trouble along the way. Maybe he'd stop in sometime and catch up with his old friend. Funny that he'd want to.

Feeling positive about the day's work and the fact that he hadn't heard one cruel remark about his family, he gunned the engine and headed north toward the river bridge. With the wind in his face and the powerful Harley rumbling beneath him, Sloan felt free.

He'd begun humming "Born to Be Wild" when a siren ripped the peaceful atmosphere behind him.

Sloan glanced in his side mirror and groaned.

Chief Dooley Crawford had spotted him.

So much for his one good day in Redemption.

Chapter Four

Annie rubbed at the headache starting between her eyebrows. "Okay, Mom, I'll talk to him again. But you know how Daddy is about his diet. He's never listened to me before."

Her dad had suffered with ulcers for years, but getting him to lay off coffee and fried foods was like asking him to cut off a limb. Her mother assumed because Annie was a registered nurse, her father would abide by her advice. The day Dooley Crawford listened to his daughter's advice or even his doctor's would be one for the record books.

"When he retires from the police force and can spend all the time he wants out at the farm with his cows and tractor and fishing ponds, he'll get better. He's under too much stress."

"You're right about that, honey," her mother said. "He's been especially agitated the last couple of weeks. The mayor wants to cut the police budget again."

Annie twisted her finger through the old-fashioned stretchy telephone cord. Lydia hadn't updated in years. "Has he said anything about Sloan Hawkins?"

She knew for a fact her father had given Sloan several speeding tickets. Which Sloan probably deserved.

"He's worried about you, Annie, as always."

Annie vacillated between exasperation and love. No wonder Dad's ulcer was acting up. "That was a long time ago, Mom. Dad needs to let it go. Sloan is here for Lydia."

"So he says."

"He is. He's really good to her. Right now, he's out back working in the flowers, determined to restore the Wedding Garden to its former grandeur because he knows how important it is to Lydia. You should see the truckloads of supplies he's bought and how hard he works."

She'd resisted staring out the windows, but every time he came inside for a glass of water or to take a break, she'd noticed.

Oh, yes, she noticed Sloan Hawkins.

"You sound as if you've forgiven him."

The unstated question gave her pause. Had she? "Time heals all wounds."

"What about Justin?"

Annie froze. "What about him?"

"Well, honey, now don't get upset, but I always wondered."

A lot of people did. "Leave Justin out of this, Mother. The subject is Daddy and his ulcer. He can relieve some of his stress by forgetting about things that happened years ago."

"He's still protective of you. Always was when it came to boys."

No, not all boys. Just Sloan. "Tell him I'm over the past and he should be, too."

"Okay, honey. I hear that tone so I'll hush up. Why don't you come to the Ladies' Auxiliary meeting Saturday? We need to decide on a fundraiser for the orphan ministry."

Annie stifled an inward sigh. Before the divorce, she'd had more time for church and community activities. Now every waking moment was work, kids, or taking care of a million and one household chores of her own.

"I'd like to, Mom, but Delaney is taking swim lessons in the mornings and Zoey Bowman invited her to a birthday party that afternoon. Plus, I need to shop for groceries and get Justin some new pants for Cheyenne's wedding. His legs are growing again." She squinted toward the clock above the stove. "Mom, I need to go. I'm still at Lydia's house. Tell Delaney I'll be late picking her up."

Following the usual goodbyes, she rang off and pushed a thumb and forefinger against her eye sockets. The headache was worse.

Sloan's hard-as-steel voice jolted her. "Don't you ever go home?"

Annie looked up to find him lounging against the entry to the kitchen. He wore frayed blue jeans with a giant hole in one knee and a sweaty green T-shirt minus any sleeves.

"Do you always have to look disreputable?"

"Clothes make the man." He flashed a set of white teeth and shoved off the door frame to indicate the fresh garden vegetables piled on the butcher-block counter. "Where did the squash come from?"

"Neighbors with bounty." She swept a hand toward the fridge. "You should look in there."

"Nice of them." He sauntered to the counter and picked up a yellow crook-necked squash. "I haven't had any fried squash since—well, in a long time."

"Now you can have all you want."

"Only if I can talk you into cooking it. I never quite got the hang of frying anything. Do you know how?"

"This is Oklahoma, Sloan. Of course I know how, except I don't because Lydia loves fried foods and she can't have them."

He frowned. "Yeah, okay. You're right." He put the squash back on the counter. "Why are you still here?"

"Lydia had too many visitors today." In spite of herself

Annie got out a bowl and knife, took the squash and began slicing. "I fell behind."

Sloan leaned a hip on the counter, standing too close for comfort. "What are you doing with that squash?"

"Frying it."

"Yeah? For me?" He sounded pleased. Surprised, too. Well, he should be. She certainly was.

"Don't make a big deal out of it. Lydia's asleep already. There are a few cucumbers and new potatoes. Want some of those, too?"

She didn't know why she felt compelled to prepare a meal for Sloan, but when he'd put Lydia's interests first without argument, some of the ice around her heart had melted. He loved Lydia even if he hadn't been around.

Sloan's face erupted in a smile. Annie's pulse skidded like tires on hot pavement. She reined in the forbidden reaction with a vicious whack at the innocent squash.

"Got any corn on the cob?" he asked.

"Sorry."

"Too bad." He brushed past her to the refrigerator, took out a cucumber and a red, ripe tomato. "I could see how tired she was, but she loves company. Always did."

Annie stopped slicing and rested the heel of her hand against the bowl. "Remember when we were kids, how Lydia would invite everyone over on summer nights to roast wieners and marshmallows?"

"I must have sharpened a million hickory sticks with my pocket knife." A dish rattled as he placed it on the counter next to her and began slicing the cucumber. The fresh, green scent rose between them.

"And after dark, we'd chase lightning bugs."

Sloan pumped his eyebrows. "And each other."

She laughed and pointed the knife at him, surprised to be able to relax this much. "That was when we were older."

"Really old, like thirteen or something." His twinkling eyes captured hers and she knew they were sharing the same memory. They were barely teens the first time he'd kissed her. Playing tag, she'd chased him around the big house into the dark area between the porch and gardens. He'd hidden, catching her by the arm as she'd raced by, yelling his name. The kiss had been short, sweet and innocent. Unlike their later relationship. And it was that later relationship—fueled by her father's objection to her dating "that Hawkins boy"—that remained between them unresolved.

She turned away from those dazzling blue eyes to reach for the flour canister. Thinking about a first kiss or any kiss with Sloan was dangerous ground.

After battering the thin yellow slices, she poured oil in a skillet and set it to heat. As she moved around the country kitchen, Sloan seemed always in the way. They bumped and jostled until she told him to sit down and let her do the cooking.

He didn't. Typical Sloan. Tell him he couldn't do something and he would die trying. He sliced the vegetables, scrubbed the potatoes, set the table with two plates, and when she protested, he just shrugged. Sloan Hawkins was pretty handy in the kitchen, which meant he'd done his own cooking. Was there not a woman in the picture?

"Your dinner is ready," she said, setting the golden squash and a plate of cold ham slices on the table.

"Yours, too." He pulled out a chair and stood behind it, waiting for her to be seated.

Fighting an unwelcome rush of attraction, she said, "I really should go."

"Come on, Annie. It's only a meal. I know you haven't eaten."

When he put it that way, she felt foolish for refusing. It *was* only a meal and she was an adult, not some silly teenager.

Justin had ball practice until dark and Mother was thrilled to have Delaney. Eating alone at home was depressing anyway. "Well, all right."

After an uncomfortable moment when she'd said grace and felt him staring at her the whole time, they began to eat.

"When did you get religious, Annie?" he asked, forking one of the crispy squash.

She didn't consider herself religious, per se. The word made her think of the scribes and Pharisees who'd condemned Christ. "I committed to Christ a few years ago, if that's what you mean. I was trying to make sense out of life, and God offered a hope I didn't have."

"Simple as that?"

"Faith *is* simple. God is good and loving, and without Him we're a mess." She laughed softly. "Sometimes I'm still a mess."

"Human nature is a mess," he said and popped a buttery new potato in his mouth. "Man, that's good. You can't buy that flavor in a store."

"Lydia has good friends. This time of year, the gardeners keep us all in great-tasting produce."

"I don't remember Redemption as being that generous."

"Because your view is skewed. Redemption is a wonderful town, filled with decent, honorable people."

He scowled at a tomato slice. "Not everyone."

"No, but most. When Joey left, I was devastated and humiliated. I'm sure a few gossips had a field day, but for the most part this little town wrapped its arms around me and helped me keep going when I wanted to give up."

"What happened? With Joey, I mean?"

Her heart lurched. Sloan didn't know it, but he was treading on dangerous ground. "Half the marriages in this country end in divorce."

"That's an excuse, not an answer."

"I could say it's none of your business."

"You could." He didn't seem the least bit offended, which was likely the reason she told him.

"Joey got tired of me, tired of the kids, tired of being married. We fought a lot after Delaney was born." She dropped her gaze to the pretty gold-rimmed china. "He started seeing other women."

Sloan's dark fingers closed over hers. "Creep. Want me to hunt him down and hurt him for you?"

The juvenile statement made her smile.

"The marriage was bumpy from the beginning. I probably shouldn't have married him at all." That was an understatement, but Joey had been eager and she had been desperate.

"Did you love him?"

"Maybe at one point." But not in the beginning, nor in the end.

She didn't say that, of course, though she experienced an interesting sense of relief, an absolution of sorts, at sharing her disastrous marriage with Sloan. She'd felt so guilty about marrying Joey while still aching for her first love. "What about you? Did you ever marry?"

She wasn't sure why she'd ventured there.

Sloan withdrew his hand and went back to his meal. "Too busy."

Annie sipped at her water, mouth suddenly dry. "Where have you been, Sloan? What have you been doing? Where did you go?"

The questions came out unbidden, but she'd wondered for so long. Why not ask now when they were both feeling comfortable and nostalgic?

Sloan chewed and swallowed, his expression bland. "I joined the army."

The answer was not what she expected. Sloan had never

once mentioned a desire to enlist. The old hurt swelled inside her. "What a weird thing to do."

His laugh was a bark. "Wasn't it?"

"Why?"

Some odd emotion flashed through his eyes but was shuttered so quickly, she could have imagined it. "A man's gotta do something with his life."

They'd had plans. Had he forgotten those? "My father said you ran away the same way your mother did."

He pretended interest in a cucumber dripping vinegar. "Is that right?"

"You tell me."

"What else did he say?" The cucumber slid off the fork and plunked onto his plate.

"He said you were in trouble with the law and ran to avoid prosecution."

"There you are, then. Just like your daddy says."

Annie heard an undertone of anger in the flip answer and wondered if there was more to the story than either her father or Sloan was willing to tell. Something in the tense set of his jaw warned her not to press the subject.

"What have you been doing since the army?"

He took a deep breath and let it out, the tension dissipating with the change in topics. "Living in Virginia. Started my own security business."

Sloan went on to describe a thriving company that protected dignitaries, heads of state, and others in need of security all over the world. Stunned, she realized Sloan Hawkins was not some thug on a motorcycle. He was a businessman, and from the sound of things, a very successful businessman.

"Wow, impressive." She couldn't quite reconcile this new Sloan with the old one.

The telephone rang.

Sloan reached over her head and took the receiver from the wall phone. "Hawkins's residence."

His face, alive and passionate about his company moments before, went flat and hard. "She is."

He handed the phone to her. "Our favorite police chief."

"Daddy?" she said into the mouthpiece.

"I tried your house. What are you still doing over there with Hawkins?"

She wasn't sixteen anymore, but her father made her feel that way sometimes. Especially since Sloan had come home. "Having dinner. Why? Do you need me for something?"

"Justin's in trouble again."

Her stomach dropped. "Oh, Dad."

Sloan came around in front of her, head tilted to one side, expression questioning. She held up one finger.

"What happened this time?"

"Deputy Risenhower caught him breaking out windows with rocks."

"Breaking windows?" She ran an exasperated hand over the top of her head. "But he's supposed to be at ball practice."

"He got kicked off the team, Annie." Her father's voice was tired. "I guess he took out his anger on the first place he encountered—Staley's drugstore. All the windows on the third floor were broken and a few on the second."

Stomach in a knot, she leaned her forehead against the heel of her hand. Staley's was a gorgeous old building on the historic register. "Oh, Justin, Justin, what am I going to do with you?"

A strong hand clasped hers and squeezed. She took one glance at Sloan, saw the compassion there and had a memory flash of him doing the same thing in high school when she'd failed a test in geometry. He'd been there for her, supporting, encouraging and always on her side.

She swallowed the heavy dose of regret mixed with

dismay. Raising a son was far more important than a test and she couldn't afford to fail.

Grateful for Sloan's support, she latched on to his strong, manly fingers. It had been a long time since she'd had anyone besides herself to lean on.

"Chuck Staley is pressing charges," her father was saying. "So my hands are tied. Says he wants to make an example out of the police chief's grandson. You'll have to pay restitution and he'll likely be on probation."

Twice before, Justin had been in scrapes and his grandfather had dealt with it. "Where is he?"

"Here at the police station. I would have taken him home but I couldn't find you." The statement was an accusation. He was upset because she was in the same house with Sloan. His ulcer would perforate if he knew they'd shared a companionable meal and conversation. If he knew they were holding hands, he'd explode.

"I'll meet you at my house in ten minutes. Okay?"

"Right. And Annie?"

"What?"

"Don't bring Hawkins."

The kid was driving her nuts.

Sloan parked his bike outside the bank and stepped up on the curb. Giant pots of red and white flowers flanked the clear glass doors of First National of Redemption.

His cash flow was running low and he was here to deal with the formalities of opening an account, but his brain was still dealing with the problem of Annie's son.

This latest incident had just about shattered her. Oh, she'd acted tough, but he knew Annie. Those big green eyes had swum with unshed tears and her voice had quivered when she was on the phone with her father.

He was disturbed at how badly he'd wanted to take her in his arms and give her the comfort she needed. He'd offered to go with her, too, to deal with the boy. Her refusal didn't surprise him, but the rejection he'd felt did.

This morning, she'd brought Justin with her to Lydia's. The kid had been his usual sulky self, but he was also more subdued. According to Annie, she was not letting him out of her sight the rest of the summer. He almost felt sorry for the boy. Whatever was eating the kid was not going to go away just because his mother was watching him every minute. The kid needed to be busy, not sitting on the couch playing video games while Annie worked to replace the broken windows. The restitution should be Justin's, not hers.

Why he should care about Annie's problems or Annie's troubled kid, he didn't know. But he did.

Stewing on that bothersome revelation, Sloan went inside the air-conditioned bank. At a teller's window, he stated his business and waited for the paperwork. Housed in a historical building dating back to 1903 like most of the town's main street, the exterior of the bank hadn't changed much since he'd been gone, but the interior boasted new glass-enclosed offices and a bevy of loan desks.

The clerk returned with the papers. Sloan signed and then took the envelope of bills, stuffing it into his jeans pocket.

As he turned to leave, an all-too-familiar voice stopped him. "Hawkins."

Sloan sighed and turned around.

Police Chief Dooley Crawford stepped away from the next teller. "Borrowing money to pay your fines?"

Annie's father was thinner than most men his age, but still tall and mean-looking. Sloan had no doubt he still evoked fear in the local teenagers.

"Been harassing any other citizens, Chief? Or am I special?"

Dooley's face hardened. "A man with your reputation needs to be real careful that he doesn't end up in jail, if you get my drift. You steer clear of my daughter. You hear?"

"Seems like I've heard that warning before."

"And last time you had sense enough to run while you could. We don't need your kind in this town."

"And what kind would that be? A law-abiding citizen come home to take care of his ailing aunt?"

Dooley sneered. "You can't fool me. You're here to cause trouble, just like your daddy and mama."

Sloan bristled. "My mama never hurt a soul."

"No? Well, she left her worthless kid to terrorize the town and keep the cops busy."

Sloan's hands fisted at his side. His years in the military and as a business leader had taught him self-discipline. And he needed every bit of it to keep from punching out the local law.

"I'm not a kid anymore, Dooley. And I don't scare. This may come as a nasty surprise—and I hope it does—but you did me a favor twelve years ago. What you meant for harm turned out to be the best thing that ever happened to me."

Dooley's narrow lips lifted in an imitation smile. "Be glad to do it again, boy."

Sloan laughed and walked away. He could feel the icy daggers of Dooley's stare against his back.

Once outside on the sidewalk, he drew in a breath of fresh, cleansing air, but his pulse pounded wildly in his ears. For those few seconds under Dooley's glare, he'd felt like a worthless teenager again.

"Sloan. Sloan Hawkins, wait up."

Sloan emitted a low growl. Someone was about to get an earful because he was in no mood for another snide remark. Not even one.

"What?" he barked, one hand on the handlebars of his bike, eager to escape as soon as possible.

Two women came toward him, toting shopping bags. He recognized one as Kitty Wainright, a former schoolmate and owner of the Redemption Motel. She'd been Kitty Bates back then, dating Dave Wainright. According to Aunt Lydia, Kitty was a widow now, Dave lost in the Middle East wars. Lousy deal. The other was a woman with ink-black hair and a cop's walk. He could spot a trained police officer a mile away.

"Sloan, this is my friend, Cheyenne Rhodes. We overheard what Chief Crawford said and we want you to know something."

Sloan nodded as politely as he could toward the women. Lydia had received an invitation to Cheyenne's upcoming wedding. An invitation that included him.

"Yeah?"

"Not everyone in Redemption agrees with what Chief Crawford just said. Most people never did."

"Is that a fact?" Sloan couldn't remember anyone but Annie and Lydia ever defending him.

"Yes, it is. Lots of folks back then talked about how Dooley had it in for you. Apparently, he can't let bygones be bygones."

Sloan relaxed a little. "Some of his animosity was well-earned."

"Well, maybe." Kitty laughed, a pretty, musical sound that lifted his mood. "But that was a long time ago when we were crazy kids. We all did goofy things, and Dooley was scared to death you were going to marry his baby girl."

Sloan kept quiet on that one. He *would* have married Annie if Dooley hadn't forced him out of town.

"Annie says you've been awesome to Lydia and to her, and that's enough for us."

Annie had said that? She'd been talking about him?

"I appreciate it. Thanks." He was too stunned to say anything else.

Kitty hitched a shopping bag higher on one arm. "Redemption is a nice town. The majority of people care about their neighbors and will do anything to help you out. Everyone is not like Chief Crawford."

Sloan's thoughts flashed to the fresh vegetables, the visitors, Mrs. Miller at the Garden Center. But those had been for Lydia, not for him, not for that Hawkins boy. Right?

"Redemption draws people, Sloan. I believe God has led you home for more reasons than your dear aunt." While he was digesting the cryptic comment, she switched gears on him. "Well, we've got to run. Weddings don't plan themselves." She and Cheyenne looked at each other and laughed. "When you get that garden fixed up, we expect an invitation to see it, okay?"

They'd heard about the garden, too?

"Yes, sure." Though he hated thinking the thoughts, he wanted the garden finished while Lydia was around to enjoy the results. "But it's taking longer than I'd like."

"If you need help, Redemption is loaded with teenagers looking for summer jobs."

And that's when Sloan had a great idea.

Justin sat slumped on the couch, staring belligerently at nothing. Annie sighed and started down the hall toward Lydia's room.

Lord, show me what to do about my son.

Instead of better behavior since the incident, he'd grown more sullen. Even Delaney couldn't get a smile out of him. Thank goodness this job with Lydia was mostly private duty for a friend or she would have been fired days ago.

Footsteps sounded on the stairs. Annie's stomach leaped.

Annoyed, she pressed a hand there and paused, waiting for Sloan to pass so they didn't have a repeat collision. She was still thinking about that moment in his arms far too much.

Sloan appeared, as deliciously disheveled as usual in faded jeans and a camo-green T-shirt, only today he'd exchanged the chain-laden boots for a pair of sneakers. He rounded the stairs, entered the living room and went to stand between Justin and the television set. After a quick, rueful glance toward Annie, he tossed a baseball mitt into Justin's lap.

The surprised boy *oomphed* and curled inward.

"What's this?" Justin picked up the gleaming new Rawlings glove and turned it over and over in his hands.

"You gonna play, you gotta learn to field a ground ball." Sloan bounced a snow-white baseball in one palm.

Justin's face closed up tighter than a clamshell. "Who said I wanted to play baseball anyway?"

"With your arm? You're kidding me, right?" Sloan lobbed the ball. Justin caught it in his bare hand.

"I got kicked off, remember?"

"Yeah, well, if you prove yourself, you can still make baseball camp next month."

Justin's posture straightened; a hopeful yearning came over him. "You talked to Coach?"

"So what if I did?" Sloan stabbed a finger at the surprised boy. "You gonna make me sorry?"

"No. I mean, I don't know." He shrugged, looking so bewildered that Annie wanted to laugh and cry at the same time.

"Come on, then. Move it. We got an hour to practice before your mother goes home. And I got a proposition for you."

Looking confused and suspicious, Justin took his sweet time unfolding all the lanky arms and legs from the couch, but Annie could feel an underlying excitement coming off her son. She wanted to hug Sloan.

"You really think I got a good arm?" Justin asked as the two of them headed for the French doors.

"No doubt about it, kid." Sloan clapped Justin on the shoulder. "You just gotta learn to use it appropriately."

Heart clutching in her chest for all that wasn't and all that might have been, Annie watched the man she'd once loved encourage her son in a way Joey never had. Justin was desperate for a man's attention, someone other than his grandfather, who alternately spoiled and ignored him.

Lord, I don't know whether to be thrilled or terrified. Give me wisdom.

As if Sloan knew she was still standing at the end of the hall staring his way with a longing too strong to ignore, he glanced back over one shoulder and winked.

Chapter Five

Annie helped Lydia from the bed to the chair next to the wide windows overlooking the gardens. The older woman was growing weaker each day and slept more than she was awake. Sloan was usually hovering in the doorway when his aunt opened her eyes, an action that pinched Annie's heart.

As she adjusted the oxygen tubing, she asked, "Would you like a snack, or something to drink? You haven't eaten much today. I have some fresh melon and strawberries."

The move from bed to chair had taken a toll. Lydia, still catching her breath, only shook her head. Until recently, she'd read or crochet while sitting up, but this week, Sloan had begun reading to her, and the beginnings of a stocking cap for the orphan ministry lay unfinished in the basket.

Lydia was determined to attend the upcoming wedding of Cheyenne Rhodes and the local vet, Trace Bowman, but after these last few days, Annie had her doubts.

"I'm not sure you should try to go Saturday."

She adjusted her patient's lap robe, fussing with it more than was necessary. Annie had come to love this woman when she was a child and she loved her even more now that they were together every day. The idea of losing her grew more and more difficult to accept. She could only imagine how Sloan was feeling.

Lydia patted her hand. "I'll be fine, honey. Stop worrying. Sloan promised to take me."

"He did?"

Lydia's chuckle turned to a cough, and another minute passed before she could speak again. "He's a good man, Annie. I think you know that in your heart. Don't be afraid of him." She nodded toward the window. "Just look out there."

Annie had resisted watching Sloan with Justin, but now she did. The lacy white curtains were drawn to the sides in a swoop, giving a full view of the backyard through the large double windows. As she observed, a lump in her throat, Sloan fired a fast grounder toward Justin. Her son crouched low, scooped up the ball and fired it back. Sloan said something and grinned. Justin's laugh seeped through the walls of the house and into Annie's soul. When was the last time she'd heard her little boy laugh with real joy?

"But why hasn't Sloan been here for you before now, Lydia? Why did he leave you alone all this time?" *And why did he run out on me when I would have stood by him no matter what he'd done?*

"Oh, honey, Sloan has always been here for me."

Annie turned from the window. "Then why haven't I seen him? Is he the invisible man?"

Lydia chuckled. "Just because he wasn't here in person doesn't mean he wasn't in contact. Who do you think took me to Italy and France and all those other places? Who do you think paid for the repairs on this old house and anything else I need? Coming home was too hard, but Sloan has never forgotten his old auntie." Lydia stopped for air, the sound ragged and harsh in the quiet room. "Now, don't you tell him I said a word. He's funny about that. Never wants credit for anything good he does."

The revelation stunned Annie. She looked out at the scene in the backyard, felt that clutching again in her chest, and wondered what else she didn't know about Sloan Hawkins.

"If you have something to tell him, Annie, don't wait too long. Time has a way of slipping by."

Annie jerked her attention from the window to Lydia, pulse bumping. "What do you mean?"

"Remember that verse in the Bible? 'The truth will set you free?' It applies in a lot of situations."

The truth. She'd lived half-truths and plain old lies for so long, Annie wasn't sure she knew the truth anymore.

She blew out a sigh. "How long have you known?"

"If you're talking about Justin, I didn't know for sure. But I've suspected for a long time. Seeing the two of them together—well, I just knew."

"Why didn't you say something?"

Lydia reached out and took her hand. "I love you, Annie girl. You're like a daughter to me. I never wanted to embarrass you or add to your hurt, and I sure never wanted to interfere in anyone else's business, but now that I'm dying, I've become a selfish old lady. I want things settled."

Tears filled Annie's eyes. "Oh, Lydia, I love you."

Lydia patted her hand. "Be kind to my boy. He's got a ways to go before all the wounds are healed. I thought I'd live to see him happy, but—"

Suddenly, Sloan's cell phone burst into song. The device rang or chirped with text messages dozens of times a day, so she was surprised to see the black rectangle lying on the windowsill in Lydia's room.

"He forgot that noisy thing when he was in earlier," Lydia said. "Do you mind taking it to him?"

Head spinning, Annie was sorry for the interruption, but she took the phone and headed outside. Never once in twelve years had she told a single person other than Joey. And though he'd assured her he didn't care, in the end he'd despised her for her sin. Would Sloan hate her, too, if he knew? Worse yet, would she lose her son? He was already a bubbling cauldron of emotional issues. Would the truth about his parentage send him over the edge?

Since the day Sloan had arrived, she'd prayed for God to show her what to do. He hadn't. With this growing appreciation of the man she'd vowed to despise, she was more perplexed than ever.

The June warmth wrapped an arm around her as she jogged down the steps toward the pair of moody males. The summer blooms that had survived in Lydia's garden were wilting, even though Sloan had made progress on ripping out weeds and unwanted mimosa sprouts. He still had a big job to do. Annie hoped Lydia would live long enough to see her garden restored.

A baseball smacked against leather.

"No way," Justin was saying.

"Won't kill you, kid. You owe your mom big-time."

Justin took the ball from the glove pocket and looked it over with undue interest. "Yeah, I know."

Annie stopped. He did?

"A man pays his debts." Sloan raised his baseball mitt, a glove as disreputable as its owner's jeans. Where had he found that? "Give me your best shot."

"Pretty brave, dude. I got heat." Justin grinned, wound up like a pro pitcher and threw hard, grunting with the effort. The ball went wide left toward the picket fence, and Sloan missed the catch. He loped to the fence and as he did, he spotted Annie standing inside the garden gate.

"Your phone," she called, waving the device overhead. By now, the caller had given up, but the message signal had beeped.

Sloan slapped at his pants pocket as though he couldn't believe he'd left the phone somewhere. The device was part of his body.

"Thanks." He under-handed the ball to Justin. "Take five, kid. Let's run my offer past your mother."

Justin's sulk returned. "Whatever."

Annie went to join them beneath the shade of a mimosa. "What offer?"

"Justin broke the windows," Sloan said. "He should pay for them himself. I offered him a job working on Aunt Lydia's garden with me. Minimum wage. Bonus if he's worth it."

Annie's heart leaped into her throat. "Seriously? You'd do that?"

"I need the help. He needs the job. Right, Justin?"

Justin allowed a shoulder hitch, eyes averted to be sure the adults knew how disinterested he was. "Sure, whatever."

A grin broke over Sloan's face. "I like this kid. Great attitude. Reminds me of someone I used to know."

The joking comment was like ice water in Annie's face. Emotions jumbled and another headache starting, she turned back to the house and her patient. She had some serious praying to do.

Sloan hated weddings.

For the dozenth time in the last hour, he adjusted the new silk tie he'd had to buy for this wedding of two people he barely knew. But his aunt asked for so little, and if attending the wedding of two friends was that important to her, he was going to see that she not only attended, but that she had a good time and was well cared for. Not that Annie wasn't hovering like a mother hen.

He grinned a little at that. She'd done everything possible to talk Lydia out of going, but his aunt had insisted, stating that she'd prayed for those two to be healed from their heartaches and joined in love, and she was not about to miss God's handiwork coming to fruition. After that, Annie had given in and begun her meticulous preparations to give Lydia the day she wanted.

So had Sloan. After a hard, sweaty day in the sunny garden with the sulky but surprisingly useful Justin, he'd come inside to shower and dress while Annie whisked the kid home to get herself ready. He liked the boy, another surprise, just as he liked the cute little Delaney, who spent most days with her grandma, but on others roamed in and out of Lydia's house with glasses of lemonade or drawings for them to admire.

Annie's kids. He plopped down on the foot of the ancient four-poster and stared at his gleaming black shoes. Their old man didn't know what he was missing. Joey needed his behind kicked for throwing Annie and the kids aside. Justin, in particular, needed his father.

With a grunt, Sloan tossed the comb on the counter. Nothing he could do about Joey's problems, or even Annie's, for that matter.

He shrugged into his suit jacket and checked himself out in the mirror one final time. A spritz of cologne and he'd do. At least he wouldn't shame his aunt, and Redemption wouldn't run backward today when they got a load of that Hawkins boy.

The radio clock gleamed red from the nightstand. Sloan grimaced. Time to get the show on the road. After straightening his tie one last time, he jogged down the stairs.

From the front entry came the sound of voices. Annie and her kids had arrived. Butterflies fluttered in his belly. He rolled his eyes at the juvenile reaction and went to greet the trio.

With the two children in front of her, Annie glanced up just as he appeared in the hallway. Dark blond hair backlit by the sunlight coming in from the overhead transom, she looked like an angel. Sloan's butterflies returned. To date, he'd only seen her dressed in work scrubs. Today she wore high heels and some kind of flowy print dress in a shade of green that drew attention to her eyes and her curvy figure. Long, dangly pearls dripped from her earlobes and a simple pearl bracelet slid up and down on one wrist. He didn't want to notice, but like a man too long in the Sahara he drank in the beautiful sight.

"Wow," he said, in spite of himself. His pulse kicked up and shot a zing of energy into his bloodstream. Annie Markham was a knockout, a woman any man would be proud to have at his side.

He bit back the reaction. All the reasons she couldn't be by *his* side rolled around in his gut until he was nauseous.

Her generous mouth widened in a smile. Was that a blush of pleasure he detected on those unforgettable cheeks? "Wow yourself. Look at you in a suit and tie."

Determined to keep a light tone in spite of the leap of longing eating a hole inside him, he rubbed his smooth jawline. "Shaved, too. What do ya think?"

"I think you look—" Sloan's confidence rose as Annie's gaze roamed over his navy blue suit and red tie. Her mouth opened and closed as if she wasn't quite sure what to say. She finally ended with "—distinguished."

"Distinguished?" He pretended hurt. "You might as well have said 'Presentable.'"

"Well, you're that, too," she answered, with a small laugh.

"What about handsome and manly and super-hunk?"

Justin interrupted with a noise of disgust. "You two are boring. Can we go now?"

"But, Justin," little Delaney said. "They do look pretty. You look pretty, too."

The boy had changed remarkably in the last couple of

hours. Somehow Annie had coaxed him into dark, crisply creased slacks and a white button-up shirt with a blue tie. His ragged sneakers had been replaced with black dress shoes, his hair was moist with hair gel, and he looked as stiff as his shoes probably felt. Sloan felt his pain.

Justin rolled his eyes in that familiar way he had of showing total disgust. "Guys aren't pretty. We dress up because women make us. Right, Sloan?"

Sloan grinned. "No comment, buddy. I don't have a death wish. Just remember what I told you. Keep your eye on the prize."

"Oh, yeah. Cake and punch."

They bumped fists. "Right."

Not to be outdone, Delaney insinuated herself between the two males. Sloan emitted a low whistle of admiration. "Let me see that dress you're wearing, Miss Delaney Doodle-bug."

She giggled. "You're silly."

Then she preened for him, spinning in a circle on her white sandals so that her skirt and her long blond hair twirled. "This was my Easter dress but I still like it. Purple is my favorite color."

No surprise there. Half the drawings she'd done for him featured some shade of purple.

"You're a beauty." He looked above her head to where Annie was standing. Their gazes connected and held.

Everything in him wanted to say "Gorgeous like your mother," but he was treading on thin ice today emotionally. No point in getting himself kicked in the teeth.

Seeing Annie dressed up for a wedding was doing weird things to him.

"We'd better get Lydia in the car and go," he said, more gruffly than he'd intended.

Annie moistened her lips and nodded. "I parked by the ramp you installed."

"Thanks for taking your car."

The comment seemed to break the tension. "I doubt she would ride on your Harley."

"Sure she would," he said, joking.

But would Annie?

Sloan hissed at the unwanted question. He and Annie were over long ago. Why were his head and his heart going crazy today?

Redemption Fellowship was humming with quiet conversation as Annie guided her two children and her patient down the aisle. Sloan pushed Lydia's wheelchair, the fingers of his hands tense against the handles. She knew he was anxious about attending church, but he hid it well behind the confident swagger that had driven her father mad and fueled her teenage crush.

Heads turned as they passed and people nodded or called out a greeting. Sloan's return greeting was almost grim. He had been defensive for so long, expecting everyone to reject him, that she wondered if he could see the admiration on the faces around them. She had always thought him the handsomest man she'd ever known, but in a dress shirt that matched his blue eyes and a red tie that accented his dark hair, he was the stuff dreams were made of. Her dreams, anyway.

But she'd learned the hard way not to be fooled by dreams.

"Is this seat okay?" the usher asked, indicating a vacant pew with access to a side exit. "You'll have the end and the door in case Miss Lydia needs to leave."

"Wild horses couldn't drag me away," Lydia answered, but her voice was frightfully weak and raspy today. The preparations alone had taken too much out of her, but though she'd argued, Annie had not been able to change her mind about attending.

With a smile, Annie said, "This is perfect."

Sloan positioned himself next to Lydia, and Delaney plopped down on his other side, whispering excitedly about the pretty lavender flowers and bows decorating the church. Needing to be near her patient, Annie sat beside her daughter with Justin at her elbow. This close she could smell Sloan's cologne—a subtle, expensively masculine mix of spice and sandalwood that had driven her to distraction in the car. She'd be salivating by the time the wedding ended if she didn't find something to take her mind off Sloan Hawkins.

Fortunately, the wedding music commenced. Traditional notes of "Amazing Grace" played on a violin accompanied the groom, the minister and the best man as they made their way to the front of the church. Annie had known Doctor Trace Bowman both personally and professionally since he'd moved to Redemption, and she had never seen him happier than in the last year since he and the darkly intense woman from Colorado had fallen in love. Today he radiated happiness as his daughter, the effervescent Zoey, made her way carefully down the aisle, strewing rose petals along the way. For a blind child, Zoey was remarkably confident, but her grandmother, Trace's mother, walked behind, one hand resting lightly on the child's shoulder.

Then the music changed and the congregation stood as a unit. A little thrill raced along Annie's arms. She loved weddings, especially this moment when the bride appeared in all her glory and the groom got that thunderstruck expression on his face.

Cheyenne, a former police officer who had overcome a terrible violent attack to become a champion to battered women, floated down the aisle on her father's arm. Her dark beauty was glorious in a long, ivory dress of simple design, her ink-black hair lying in wispy layers on her bare shoulders.

The ceremony began and Annie couldn't help watching the

faces of the guests. Half the town was here. Miriam and Hank Martinelli from the Sugar Shack—who had, no doubt, created the cake du jour—exchanged frequent glances that made Annie smile. The couple had been married for years, but their devotion burned bright.

Kitty Wainright, the maid of honor, sniffled. Jace Carter, a local building contractor, was watching the pretty motel owner with such intensity, Annie began to wonder. Did Kitty have an admirer? If she did, would she ever let go of her memories and take a chance on love again?

Lydia coughed and Annie's attention snapped to her, but Sloan had leaned forward, blocking her view. After a moment, he sat back and she could see that her patient was all right.

She turned her attention back to the ceremony. Trace and Cheyenne, gazing at each other with trust and adoration, repeated their vows. A hot knot tightened in Annie's chest—a knot of yearning to love and be loved forever. Tears gathered in her eyes. She always cried at weddings but today with the memories of the past sitting an arm's length away, the emotion was raw.

Despite her determination not to, she sneaked a peak around her daughter. Sloan's jaw was hard as granite and he swallowed often, a sign she recognized as emotion. Was Sloan feeling it, too? This painful case of what-might-have-been? What if Sloan had never left town? What if they had married? Would they have stood before the church with friends and family surrounding them, breathing in the scent of gardenias and candle smoke?

Sloan chose that moment to glance her way and caught her staring. She held on to his gaze, trying to read him, but his blue eyes burned with some emotion she couldn't identify. A muscle twitched in his cheek, and after a moment when Annie thought her heart would jump right out of her chest, he rotated toward Lydia and whispered something.

Blinking back tears, Annie looked down at the tissue she'd twisted to bits in her lap.

What a foolish woman she was. Sloan was here for Lydia, not for her. The emotional wedding atmosphere had put sappy, nostalgic thoughts in her head. That was all.

Sloan Hawkins had left of his own free will and never looked back, giving her no thought or consideration. The last thing she and her children needed was another man they couldn't count on.

Chapter Six

"Hey, Sloan, can I ask you something?"

Sloan paused in digging a hickory scrub out of Lydia's roses to lean on his shovel. Something had been eating at the kid all morning. Something was eating at him, too, and her name was Annie, which was part of the reason he and Justin were out here in the hottest part of the day. Ever since the wedding, when Annie had looked at him with tears floating in those big green eyes, he'd known he was in more trouble than Chief Dooley could ever manufacture.

She'd nearly melted him with that look, and though he knew better than to read anything into it, he couldn't stop thinking about it. He also couldn't stop thinking about Annie and Joey standing before a preacher somewhere getting married. His gut churned every time that picture entered his head. Like now.

With more force than necessary, he tossed the shovel aside and whipped off dirty leather gloves to backhand a drenched brow.

"Sure," he said to Justin. "Take five. Grab some water."

Justin set aside the bag of fertilizer he was dumping into

a wheelbarrow and removed his gloves, slapping them on the side of his leg the way Sloan had. The boy, though thin and lanky, was surprisingly strong for an eleven-year-old. His face dripped with sweat and his white T-shirt would never see clean again. Sloan figured it was good for him to sweat out some of that anger festering in him like poison.

Justin tossed him a bottle of water from the small ice chest Sloan kept handy and headed for the back of the garden and the shade of huge drooping oak branches.

Sloan opened the bottle of water and guzzled half of it, letting the cold liquid drip down his chin onto his steaming chest.

Suddenly, his skin prickled and it had nothing to do with the cold water. Annie must be looking out the window again. Bottle to his lips, he glanced toward the house, saw her there and hitched his chin. She wiggled her fingers and Sloan felt a goofy lift in his belly.

Man. He was messed up. She was waving at her kid, not at him. Annie was worried sick about the boy and probably scared that Sloan Hawkins was a bad influence.

"You coming or you gonna stare at my mom?"

Sloan grunted. Smart-aleck kid. He guzzled the rest of the water, tossed the empty onto the growing stack next to the fence, grabbed another bottle and followed Justin to the shade.

The kid was doing all right. Even Annie acknowledged as much. After the initial few days when his smooth hands had blistered on the end of a shovel and he'd griped about the heat, the work and the injustice in the world, the boy had come around. Sloan figured most of the whining was posturing and now that he had it out of his system, they were getting along pretty well. Justin wasn't afraid to work and didn't really mind the dirt and heat no matter how much he griped—which wasn't much the last few days.

Together they collapsed beneath the huge, ancient oaks,

leaning their backs against the rough bark of opposite trees. Both lifted their knees and dangled their drinks over one. Sloan thought it was kind of funny the way Justin imitated him. Funny and a little worrisome. What kind of role model was Sloan Hawkins?

He removed his shades and hung them on the neck of his T-shirt. Justin, he noticed, did the same.

Sloan laughed and pointed his water bottle at the rings of dirt around the boy's eyes. "Raccoon."

Justin snickered. "You, too. Your face is brown as dirt and your eyes are white."

"Handsome dudes, too. Can't keep the women off."

The boy allowed a tiny smile but Sloan could see he had something on his mind. "So, what's up? Something bothering you?"

"Yeah." He took a swig of water and stared toward the house. Sloan followed the gaze. Annie had disappeared. "I was wondering something."

"Spit it out. I'm listening." Sloan swigged at his bottle, casual-like, careful not to press the kid or look at him while he gathered the courage to ask whatever was on his mind.

Justin tossed a dirt clod and watched it break against a tree trunk. When the small patter of sound subsided he said, "Are you my real father?"

Sloan spit water halfway across the garden. Whoa! Where had that come from? He'd expected the kid to ask him about life or girls or paying restitution for his crime. Not this. Never this.

Adrenaline jacked into his bloodstream like jet fuel. Sloan wanted to get up and run.

He took a minute to think, to breathe, to get his heart back in his chest. Annie would kick him if he handled this wrong. He'd kick himself.

Think, Hawkins. Do it right. The kid deserved a legitimate answer, not some half-truth or platitude. If he was old enough to ask, he was old enough to know.

Besides, hadn't he wondered the same thing?

Treading lightly to test the waters, Sloan said, "What makes you ask?"

Justin's expression darkened. "Just tell me. Are you? I hope you are because I hate my old man."

Whoa. So much for testing the waters. He'd just waded out into the deep with a rock around his neck.

He took his time, leaned back against the rough bark of the oak, propped a foot, and dangled the water bottle over one knee.

He knew from bad experience the kid didn't need to go through life with unanswered questions hanging over him like a guillotine, waiting to slice him in two at every turn. If Justin had the question inside him, he deserved an answer.

"I'm a straight shooter, Justin. So here it is, as straight as I can give you."

The tension radiating off the boy was painful to watch. "Yeah? Are you?"

"I don't know."

Justin's head jerked once. "So you could be."

Sloan figured he'd let that one go. The boy wasn't stupid. "If this is eating you up, you should talk to your mom. She should be the one to answer a question this important."

The silence told Sloan what the boy thought about that suggestion.

Okay, try again. This was way too crucial to the kid's mental health to leave it dangling.

"Want to tell me where you got this idea? Ronnie Prine, maybe?"

"Maybe."

"Might as well tell me. There aren't any secrets between us now." He held the boy's eyes, waiting for the acknowledgment to sink in. Justin *could* be his son. The possibility was there, however slight.

At the thought seeping in like rainwater through cracked walls, Sloan felt a strange mix of hope and despair. What if Justin *was* his son?

Justin's Adam's apple bobbed. He fiddled with the label on the bottle. "Ronnie's a creep. His mom said you and my mom…back in high school…well, you know."

Sloan huffed one hard, disgusted huff. Yes, he knew.

"Will it help to know I loved her?"

Justin's head jerked up and his eyes gleamed suspiciously damp. "Did you? Really?"

"Yeah," Sloan said, almost grimly. The kid was killing him. "Really."

"What happened?"

Ah, now, there was a slippery slope. "Your granddad didn't like me. I joined the military." Close enough to the truth.

"He still hates you. I heard him griping at Mom about you."

The heaviness in Sloan's chest expanded. Some things never changed. No matter how he'd felt or was feeling about Annie now, Dooley Crawford would stand in the way. He'd make Annie miserable again, as he'd done before. There was no way Sloan was going to ask her to choose. She had enough to deal with.

"Talk to me about your dad." When Justin just stared at him, he said. "Joey. Why do you say you hate him?"

"He's a jerk. He cheated on Mom."

"You get that from Ronnie Prine, too?"

The kid gave a short mirthless laugh. "Everybody knew but Mom. Even me. Kids talk. They teased me."

Not good. No wonder the kid was boiling on the inside. "You know what your dad did was wrong, don't you? Your mother is a good woman. She deserved better than that."

Justin managed an embarrassed grin. "I'm not a little kid. I know about…that kind of stuff."

Sloan remembered thinking the same thing the night his mother left.

"Your mom's a real special woman. A man lucky enough to marry her should treat her like a queen." He bumped the boy's knee. "Her son should treat her that way, too. She deserves your best."

"You gonna tell her? I mean, about what I asked you?"

"I think I should, don't you?"

Head down, Justin rubbed a hand over his damp hair. "If you do, will you tell me what she says?"

The implication of his little chat with Justin rocked Sloan's world. He wasn't sure what he felt. Pure terror, for certain, but also a kind of longing he couldn't fathom.

What would he do if this was his son? If he were a father? He, who was tormented with Clayton Hawkins's blood running in his veins, was now tormented by the thought that he may have abandoned his kid the way his mother had abandoned him.

Maybe he was as worthless as Dooley claimed. Maybe he was a bad seed.

But then where did that leave Justin?

Annie was vacuuming the living room when Sloan came storming in with thunder in his face and yanked the electric cord from the wall. The loud motor fell to a whine and then ceased.

"We gotta talk."

Her heart bumped, the way it did every time Sloan came striding in with that swagger and the heat of summer steaming off his tanned skin. He was dirty from head to toe, his face streaked with sweat and dust, and his T-shirt clung to his skin. He filled the room with his presence, dark and intense and determined.

She wanted to joke and ask if he'd found a daffodil bulb where the rhododendron should be, but the tension in his body told her this was serious.

Her thoughts went to her child. She swung toward the window. "Where's Justin? Is he all right?"

Sloan touched her arm. "He's fine. I gave him twenty bucks and sent him uptown for a six-pack of Gatorade and something to snack on."

"Walking?"

"He has legs."

"But he's alone." She hadn't planned to let him out of her sight. "What if he gets into more trouble?"

Sloan fisted his hands on his hips. "He won't."

Lord forgive her. Sloan had more confidence in Justin than she did.

"Okay, talk. I'm listening." She pulled the electric cord up and began to wrap it around the vacuum's hooks.

Sloan's hand stopped her. "Leave it. Please."

It was the *please* that got to her. She dropped the cord and then wondered what to do with her hands. She couldn't remember feeling awkward with Sloan before but as he stood there, with something serious on his mind and his eyes shooting blue laser fire, she had the strangest urge to bolt while she could.

"I have a feeling I'm going to be upset."

"That's not my intention, Annie, but Justin asked me a question today that I can't answer."

Annie's heart began to race. She gripped the handle of the upright vacuum cleaner. "What did he ask?"

Sloan studied her face as if he wasn't sure how to say what was on his mind. That muscle below his eyes ticked and she fought the need to stroke the spot in reassurance as she'd done long ago. But Sloan Hawkins was a man now, not a broken boy. He no more needed her than he needed another Harley.

"Sloan?" she said, hearing the anxiety in her voice. "What did he ask?"

As if the words were heavy, Sloan's chest rose and fell in a quick huff of air. "He wants to know if he's my son."

Annie's hand went to her lips, but the gasp escaped anyway. This was the last thing she expected to hear.

"He's too young to ask questions like that."

"No, he's not, Annie. Trust me. He knows what he's asking, but he's too young to deal with it on his own."

"Where did he get such an idea in the first place? He couldn't have come up with that by himself."

"Think about it. Ronnie Prine." Sloan's jaw was tight.

"So that's why he and Ronnie are constantly fighting?"

"Partly. Roberta always had a big mouth and she spread trouble like fertilizer."

Everything made sense now. Annie felt like the worst mother on earth. Justin had been defending her honor in the only way an eleven-year-old knew how. No wonder he was angry and confused.

"Roberta never liked me," she said. "She was jealous. She had a crush on you. Did you know that?"

Sloan's expression was horrified. "You have to be kidding."

"I'm not. A woman scorned is a dangerous thing." Roberta wasn't the only girl who'd noticed Sloan Hawkins, but he'd been clueless of his appeal. He'd been a one-woman man and that woman had been Annie.

He rubbed a hand down his face, further smearing the dust and dirt. "You still haven't answered the question. He needs to know and so do I. Is Justin my son?"

It was almost a relief to have this out in the open at long last. Lydia's urging ringing in her head, Annie said the only thing she could. "Yes."

With a groan, Sloan collapsed on the sofa and dropped his head in his hands. "How much do you hate me?"

Hot emotion burned inside her. Annie eased down next to him, so terribly tempted to touch him, and yet she resisted. "Not nearly enough."

He made a small huffing sound. "God help me."

"He will. How do you think I got through the hardest time of my life?"

"I can't even imagine."

"I wanted him, Sloan, from the moment I knew I was pregnant." She'd wanted Sloan, too, the pair of them together as man and wife, raising the child they'd made together.

"Why didn't you tell me?"

"I never had the chance. You know I would have." The love they'd shared had been real, even though they were too young and foolish to handle it properly.

He nodded, lifting his head to stare out the windows. "Yes, I know. We have to tell him."

"No."

"I promised him, Annie, and he needs the facts, not wild and hurtful rumors. He already suspects and it's tearing him up. Do you have any idea what it's like to live with gossip and suspicions but never really know the truth?"

She had no doubt he was thinking of his mother. Since he was Justin's age, Sloan had wondered why Joni Hawkins had left, where she'd gone, or if she would ever return. Annie, too, had lived with that kind of wondering after Sloan had left and she understood how painful the not knowing could be. At least she'd had her father's word that Sloan was gone for good. Sloan had had nothing but an older aunt who'd loved him and taken him in.

"'The truth shall set you free,'" she said softly, realizing the words were true. She felt freer in the last few minutes of truth than she'd felt for years.

Sloan turned to look at her. "What?"

"Something Lydia told me from the Bible. The truth will set you free."

"She said that to me the other day when I was reading to her. Think she was preparing us for this?"

More than once, she'd seen him sitting by Lydia's bed, reading the worn black Bible. The sight had caused a hitch in her heart. "Yes, I do. She knew about Justin."

Annie figured half the town suspected but no one had ever said a word—until now.

Sloan got up and went to the window, his back to her. He was quiet for a while and she wondered what was churning inside that complicated head of his.

"I have money," he said, pivoting suddenly. "Whatever you need."

Hand to her chest, Annie reeled back against the floral sofa cushions, stunned and hurt. "I don't want your money. Is that what you think? That you can buy twelve years with a check?"

His jaw hardened. "That's not what I meant."

"What *did* you mean? You drove away and left me. I had your baby. Money doesn't fix that."

Sloan blew out a breath of frustration. "I didn't know about him."

"Which is the only reason I didn't throw you out of here the day you roared up on that terrifying Harley. I had planned to tell you about the baby the night of the prom."

Sloan's eyes dropped shut. His lips barely moved. "The night I left."

The old wound rose up inside her and tears pressed against the back of her eyelids. She'd been so excited that day. Like all the other girls, she'd had her nails and hair done, she'd bought the perfect dress, and she had the most perfect date in town. Even though her belly had fluttered with the news growing inside, she'd excitedly planned exactly how and when to tell Sloan. In her overly romantic teenage mind, her father could no longer keep her and Sloan apart. Now that there was a baby, they could be married. But something happened that day that she'd never fully understood, and she'd been stood up at the senior prom. Sloan had gotten into trouble with the law and left town without a word.

"Why, Sloan? Why didn't you at least call me? I would have stood by you no matter what you'd done."

The blue eyes, blazing a moment ago, shuttered. "I couldn't."

"Why?" Hadn't he loved her enough to give her that one thing? If he would only explain, maybe this terrible ache would go away forever.

But he didn't. Abruptly, he pushed off the couch. "I'm going to tell him, Annie. It would be better if we do it together but one way or another, he's going to know the truth."

Sloan figured he was the most worthless human being that ever lived. He kick-started the Harley and roared away from the big Victorian, the urge to find Dooley Crawford and break his nose eating a hole in him.

Dooley must have known or suspected that the relationship between him and Annie had gone too far. He must have. There was no other explanation for the purposeful and well-timed railroading Sloan had gotten at the police chief's hands.

He sped past the town square where a city employee, Jim Barta, he thought, was mowing the grass. The green smell of summer drifted on the air. He lifted an index finger to wave at Tooney Deer and then again when Popbottle Jones and G.I. Jack sauntered out of the Sugar Shack.

After another ten minutes of arguing, Annie had finally

agreed to talk to Justin. Alone. For Justin's sake, she'd claimed. But he knew better.

Annie didn't want him involved. She didn't want him to be part of her son's life. *His* son. He bit down on his back teeth hard enough to dislocate his jaw.

Her rejection cut him to the bone and he was bleeding inside.

He revved the motorcycle, winding out the engine until it whined. Let Dooley catch him today and there would be trouble the old chief couldn't handle. Sloan needed to be alone and he needed to think.

By the time he reached Redemption River Bridge, some of his fury had subsided. Wind and a wild ride usually calmed him down, and the fresh breeze from the big, muddy river cleared his head.

He parked the bike in the shade of a willow just off the road and made his way down the riverbank, along a well-worn path past blackberry bushes and more willows. When he reached bottom, he doubled back toward the bridge and stepped beneath it into the shade. The river was low this time of year, allowing a natural shelter beneath the bridge, although at times the spot was flooded. Today the area was littered with cans and a few cigarette butts, a sure sign that teenagers still frequented the place as he and Annie and their friends once had.

Sliding his back against the cool concrete, Sloan sat down on one of the many piles of rocks and listened to the water lap the edges. The rocks were moist and cool, and the sounds and smells familiar even though he'd been gone so long.

The day he'd learned his mother had disappeared, Chief Dooley had taken him to Lydia's house. Scared and confused, he'd run back to his mother's rental, searching for her. Then he'd gone to the diner where she'd worked. When the people there looked at him with pity, he'd run here to the river.

In his mind's eye, he saw himself as a boy—out of breath,

crying, pounding the walls of this bridge with his fists. Annie had found him here and cried with him. Later, she'd walked him back to Aunt Lydia's and stayed for cookies and milk.

Sloan pressed a fist to his mouth. He'd loved Annie for so long he didn't know how to stop.

Now that they had a son together, he was forever bound to her. He laughed, a bitter sound. He'd always been bound to Annie Crawford Markham. Justin only tightened the knot.

He tilted his head back against the cool stone wall and looked up. Colorful graffiti stared back at him, some carved, some spray-painted and some in marker. Somewhere up there he'd written his and Annie's names and the word *forever.*

He was amazed to discover it was true. He'd loved her forever. Still did. And that truth didn't make him free. It made him mad. It broke him in two.

Annie had borne him a son. His whole body ached to think of what she must have endured in the days after discovering he'd left town. Yet, Annie had found a way to care for his baby. Even though she'd been a teenager, with strength and love she'd held her head up and forged ahead with life for the sake of their child.

Part of him had longed to ask if she'd loved Joey Markham, but he was afraid of the answer. He figured she had. Sloan Hawkins had been a moment of madness in her young life, and when she'd come to her senses, Annie had chosen the boy her father always wanted for her. A boy who had openly pursued Annie even while she was dating Sloan. The fact that Joey and Annie had married within two months of Sloan's departure was now much more significant.

Sloan shucked off his boots, and then emptied his pockets into them and set the footwear side by side on a rock. No one was around. The river was calm. A long time ago, he'd skinny-dipped in this river. Today, he'd settle for a swim. From local history, he knew the area under the bridge was once a low-water crossing but farther along, the river deepened. He stepped into the water and started walking in that direction.

Cold, red water swirled around his calves and quickly moved up to his knees. Five strides later, he dove under.

The shock of cold against his hot skin made his nerve endings screech and he came up shaking his head. "Brrr."

Water sluiced down his face. Back in Virginia, he had a pool. Every day he made himself swim laps whether he wanted to or not. All his employees were required to remain in top condition and he couldn't ask less of himself. But here in Redemption, he'd not had that opportunity. Still, his muscles knew the rhythm and he stroked the hundred yards toward the far bank.

As he came up the muddy, rocky incline, legs sluggish from the weight of wet jeans, a voice called out.

"Ahoy there, Sloan Hawkins."

An old man dressed in cast-off, mismatched clothes skidded down the embankment toward him. Sloan's heart sank. He'd wanted to be alone, but there was no way he'd be rude to Popbottle Jones. The man was a good friend to Aunt Lydia. Yesterday he'd brought her flowers, an action that had made Annie tear up and hurry inside the house.

Sloan lifted a hand. "Mr. Jones."

"A fine day for a swim. How's the water?"

"Cold. Muddy. Invigorating." Sloan shoved his sopping hair back from his forehead. "Where's your partner?"

"G.I.? He had some errands to run, which was just as well since I wanted to speak with you alone."

"Yeah?" Sloan's guard went up. Popbottle had seen him pass through town, guessed his destination, and followed for a reason. This was not a casual encounter.

"How is your aunt today?"

His guard fell. "Not well. The wedding took a heavy toll. She's hardly been out of bed since."

Until now, she'd taken her meals with him and occasionally sat on the veranda to watch him work in her gardens. She was thrilled about restoring the Wedding Garden to its former glory, and Sloan had wanted more than anything to make that happen while she was alive to see it. But since the wedding she only shuffled back and forth to the bathroom, and that with Annie's assistance.

"I did my best to dissuade her from attending." Popbottle's jowls sagged, though a soft smile touched his eyes. "But she *did* look radiant."

"She's weaker every day." Sloan hated the admission, but in his career he'd learned to be a realist. Facts were facts. His auntie was fading away with the summer.

He bent to press some of the water from his pants legs. The red liquid slid over his feet like diluted blood.

"She's worried about you."

Sloan straightened. "I don't want her to be."

"She can't help it. And as you well know, worrying is not good for her heart."

"Maybe I should go back to Virginia." But Sloan knew he wouldn't. He couldn't bear to leave her, knowing as he did that she would not be here if he returned. Right now, with the issue of Justin simmering like the Middle East, he wasn't going anywhere.

"Regardless of your location, my boy, she would still be concerned. You are the child she never had."

The thought pinched a hole in Sloan's chest. His aunt Lydia had never married though she had many friends and was well-loved in the community. To his way of thinking, her acceptance was all that kept Clayton Hawkins's boy from being a total outcast. She'd taken in her brother's son and loved him as her own, and Sloan would carry that love with him to the grave. "I don't know how to stop her from worrying. If I did, I would do it in a heartbeat."

Popbottle placed a hand on his shoulder. "She always had hopes for you and Annie."

Sloan grunted. "That's not happening."

"Yet you are undoubtedly in love with our kind and lovely nurse."

Well, happy day, Sloan thought sarcastically. Did the whole world know he was an idiot who couldn't stop loving a woman who was far too good for him? A woman he'd wronged so completely that there was no going back?

"And you're in love with my aunt."

The old man removed a brimmed hat that Annie would term "disreputable" and scratched at the tuft of gray hair. "Your aunt and I have been friends for a long time, but the topic of consideration this day is you, my boy. You've been in a turmoil your entire life, most of which was not your fault, but only you have the ability to end it."

"You sound like Aunt Lydia."

"She's a wise woman who knows God is the answer to all life's questions."

"God can't change the past."

"No, but He can change your future."

Sloan found himself listening intently. Lydia's Bible readings had him thinking more about God, about her steadfast faith.

"My boots are under the bridge," he said. "Walk over with me?"

"Certainly. Old legs need exercise."

Soft, red clay squished between Sloan's toes as he and Popbottle covered the fifty yards back to the bridge.

"I never gave God much thought, I guess," Sloan admitted

as they reached the structure and he stood aside to allow the older man to enter the shady area first.

"Ah, much cooler here." Popbottle Jones pinched the crease of his aged pants as if they were a tuxedo, gingerly settled on the narrow ledge, and continued the thread of conversation. "Trusting God won't solve all the issues with which you must contend, my boy, but knowing that someone greater and wiser than you is in charge gives you a peace." He tapped his chest. "In here. An assurance that everything is going to work out for your good."

"I sure don't have that." Never had. Sloan perched on his rock and reached for his boots. "The preacher invited me for coffee the other day."

He'd been surprised out of his mind, too. A Redemption preacher wanting to associate with him.

As if he'd heard his thoughts, Popbottle said, "Do you know the story of this town and its founder?"

Sloan swished his muddy feet in the shallow water and dried them with his socks.

"You can't grow up in Redemption without hearing about Jonas Case."

The reformed gunslinger had founded the small town during the Land Run of 1889 as a refuge for men like himself who wanted to change. Funny how Sloan had never thought about that. The town was created for bad boys and criminals, men struggling with their pasts, men with guts full of regret.

Men like him.

He shoved his foot into a boot.

"I often stand upon the riverbanks," Popbottle was saying as he motioned toward the well-traveled shoreline, "and think about the sermons preached here when the town was a tent city and settlers clung to God as their only hope for a new life." The old man slid a glance his way. "God is still the only hope, you know."

While Sloan wrestled with the idea, his cell phone played his latest download. The security business didn't stop just because he was half a country away.

With a nod of apology to the older gentleman, he flipped open the device and said, "Hawkins."

"Sloan?"

"Annie?" His stomach took a dive. "What's wrong? Is it Lydia?"

"No, no, Lydia is…the same."

Sloan's tense shoulders relaxed. He gave the suddenly stricken Mr. Jones a glance of reassurance. Whether the old guy wanted to admit it or not, he was in love with Lydia. The puzzle was why he'd never done anything about it.

"Justin, then?" Had the boy gone crazy with the news that Sloan was his father and done something worse than breaking windows?

"Yes. Justin." There was a pause while Sloan's pulse rattled in his ears. "I changed my mind, Sloan."

"That's not an option."

"I can't do this."

Sloan clenched his teeth. He didn't want to discuss the circumstances of Justin's birth in front of Popbottle, but Justin was going to learn the truth, one way or the other. Preferably from people he knew and trusted instead of someone like Roberta Prine.

"Are you still at Lydia's?"

"Yes."

"Hang tight. I'm on my way."

Chapter Seven

Annie heard the rumble of a Harley. Sloan was here.

She dried her hands and hung the rose-colored hand towel carefully over the rack before going to greet him.

By the time she reached the living room, Sloan had come inside.

She stopped to stare. "What happened to you?"

His clothes were wrinkled and damp and his hair was a windblown mess.

His eyebrow went up in a comical expression. "Took a little swim."

She couldn't help herself. She grinned. Taking an impromptu dip was exactly like the Sloan of old. "How was it?"

He grinned back. "Great. Wanna go next time?"

The thought of being free and confident enough as a responsible adult to jump into the Redemption River in jeans and a T-shirt was almost beyond her now. When had she become so stodgy?

"So, what's up?" he asked, tossing his sunglasses onto an end table. "Where's Justin?"

"After you left, Dad came by. I sent Justin home with him."

Sloan's face closed up tight, but his words were sarcastic. "Sorry I missed him."

"He said the same thing."

"Yeah? What else did he say?"

"Sloan, please. Can't we leave my dad out of this?"

"Never have. Why start now?"

He was getting angry, and that was the last thing Annie intended.

"Well, since you're already mad, you might as well know. He left a message for you."

Sloan laughed, but the sound was not cheerful. "See? I told you he loves me. A love note, I'm sure."

"He said you should slow down when riding through town."

"Hmm. That doesn't sound like the chief. What were his exact words?"

She sighed. He was determined to get his hackles up. "He said if you blew through town like that again, the two of you would be spending time together at the jail."

"That's my boy. Gotta appreciate consistency." His jaw ticked and his eyes blazed. This was not the way she wanted to start this discussion.

"Will you stop? We have far more important things to discuss than my overzealous father."

The fight went out of him. "You're right. I'm sorry." He reached for her hand. "Really. I'm sorry. I promised myself not to let your father rile me anymore. The bad blood between me and him is not your fault or your problem."

Annie's insides ricocheted with emotion. She loved her dad and couldn't understand why the two of them couldn't get along. But with Sloan holding her hand and staring earnestly into her eyes, she couldn't think of anyone but him.

Lord help her, she didn't want to fall in love with Sloan

again. He had a business and a home and a life in Virginia. He'd long ago washed his hands of her and Redemption.

But they had a child together.

As soon as the thought came, shame followed. She hadn't used Justin to hold Sloan then and she wouldn't use him now.

"We need to talk," she managed.

"I thought we did that already and you agreed to tell Justin about me and him."

"We did, but I just can't." She drew her hand away and the loss went clear to the toes of her sensible shoes. "Not by myself."

Sloan's demeanor changed. He went on full alert. "Hold that thought while I look in on Aunt Lydia."

"I just came out of her room. She's asleep again."

But he turned and disappeared down the long hall anyway. He was completely devoted to his dying aunt, a fact that played havoc with Annie's long-held opinion of irresponsible Sloan Hawkins. In fact, many things about the adult Sloan did not fit her mind-set. Even though he rode a Harley, drove too fast and wore those wretched jeans, he was a dedicated nephew and an obviously successful businessman. That was a shocker in itself, but it was his desire to help Justin that kept Annie awake at night. A desire that had begun even before he knew her son was also his.

Confused and troubled, Annie fidgeted while waiting for Sloan to return. She moved a bowl of rose-scented potpourri, wiped the dust off the TV, straightened a tapestry throw pillow.

She was terrified of telling Justin about his paternity. What if the boy lost all respect for her? He already had enough issues in that department since Joey's betrayal. Sometimes Justin blamed Joey. Other times he blamed himself and even though self-blame was irrational, she didn't know how to comfort him. What if the knowledge of his mother's mistakes drove him so far away she couldn't reach him?

A pensive Sloan ambled back into the living room. "I went in, but she didn't wake up."

The ache of sorrow pulled at Annie. As a nurse, she knew her patient's heart would not go on much longer. As a friend, she pleaded with God to make Lydia well.

"Let's go out on the veranda. I made some iced tea." She got them both a glass and followed Sloan to the wicker furniture. Hot sun lit the open areas of the fenced backyard, but the shady covered porch, built to encourage a breeze, was cool. "The garden is coming along. I'm really impressed with your expertise. Couples will want to be married here again when you're finished."

He and Justin had cleaned and repaired the winding pathway of stone down the center of the garden. On either side of the path, they were planting an array of flowers and bushes to keep the blooms constant. Even now, ever-blooming lavender hung its head over the pathway and released a sweet scent on the wind.

"Credit Mrs. Miller at the plant farm and some sage advice from Aunt Lydia." Sloan sipped his tea. "And the photos she kept of weddings. I just hope we can finish the work in time."

Annie didn't need to ask what he meant.

"Justin's learning a lot from you. Last night, I heard him explaining the details of propagating chrysanthemums." Fingers stroking the cold, damp glass, Annie laughed softly at the memory. "Delaney pretended to be fascinated." And Justin had puffed up with pride at his newfound knowledge.

"He's got a mind like a steel trap. Never forgets anything. You should watch him with the plants. He treats them like babies. I think the kid's a natural."

Annie listened in gratitude as Sloan spoke with pride about their son. She knew she'd made the right decision. "Will you help me tell him?"

Sloan's gaze snapped to hers. "You know I will. What changed your mind?"

"A lot of things. After you stormed out of here and I calmed down, I talked to Lydia. And I prayed about it."

Those blue irises burned with intensity. "Did God answer?"

Sloan wasn't being flip or sarcastic. Annie's heart lifted with hope that Redemption's bad boy would allow God to smooth the rough edges of his life as He'd done hers. She was a long way from perfect, but faith in God had given her a solid footing when life was crumbling around her.

"Yes, He did." The tea glass clinked as she set it on the round patio table. "Oh, not in an audible voice, but he brought some things to mind that helped me decide."

"Such as?" He drank deeply of his tea and set the glass carefully next to hers. Sloan might pretend casual indifference but his body language gave him away.

"Justin didn't pose the question to me. He asked you. He came to *you*, Sloan. I think that has to be significant. He wanted you to help figure things out, not me."

Sloan reached for the glass again but didn't drink. "Kids aren't always comfortable talking to their parents. Maybe he was embarrassed. Or maybe he didn't want to embarrass you, especially if the rumor was wrong."

"Or maybe he trusts you more." Her stomach ached to believe such a thing. "Things have been shaky between Justin and me since Joey left."

"Annie, he trusts you. He loves you. But right now, he's an angry kid who doesn't know what to do with his feelings. He even said he hates Joey."

Annie gnawed at her bottom lip. He'd said the same thing to her more than once. "I know."

"Was Joey—" Sloan's fingers flexed against the glass "—abusive?"

Joey had been a lot of things, but Annie thanked God he'd never hurt any of them physically. "No, never. He mostly ignored Justin, but he did the same with Delaney. Joey had his business, his friends. His family came last."

"That stinks."

"Yes, it does."

"Did he know that Justin wasn't his?"

"Yes. I made a lot of mistakes, Sloan, but not that one. Joey was the one person I told."

A muscle along one cheekbone jerked. "Why him?"

Not for the reasons you probably think.

"Joey came to my house the day after you left. He said he'd always loved me and wanted to be there for me." She shrugged, remembering the shattered young girl she'd been. "He said all the right things, the things I needed to hear that day. I was heartbroken and scared and I blurted out the truth. He said he didn't care. He would marry me anyway."

"And he did."

"Yes. But afterward when I began to show, he seemed embarrassed by the pregnancy. When anyone congratulated him on becoming a father, he would smile and go through the motions, but I could tell he was upset. He grew distant even before Justin's arrival. Later, when Delaney was born, I thought things would be different. They weren't. While I was in the hospital giving birth, he was with his girlfriend."

She didn't know why she'd felt compelled to tell Sloan that humiliating piece of information.

Sloan's face was blank, so she wasn't sure what he was thinking. Did he hate her for marrying Joey? Did he understand at all what she'd gone through? Did he even care?

"No wonder the kid is angry."

Something warm and sweet turned over inside Annie and she fought it, knowing the feeling was for Sloan. At the least, she should avoid this man like the flu, not be leaning on his empathy. She still didn't understand why he'd left without a word, nor had he made any effort to explain himself. Wasn't that a sign that he had never really cared?

The mother in her rose to the surface. She was not the important one here. Justin was. She could put her own heartaches aside for the sake of her child. *Their* child.

"I don't know what to do anymore." She'd spent so much time praying for Justin, her knees were sore. If God didn't give her an answer soon, she'd be crazy. "Now I'm scared of losing him completely."

Sloan reached for her hand and tucked it against his knee. Her pulse jumped, but she made no attempt to pull away.

"Eleven is a vulnerable age," he said. "What happens then can make or break you."

She suspected he was thinking of his own experience. Losing his mother had been a powerful turning point. "You turned out all right."

He gave a short, bitter laugh. "Did I? Then why have I spent my entire adult life without a relationship with my son? Why wasn't I smart enough to consider you might be pregnant when I left?"

"Beating yourself up isn't going to resolve anything. Regardless of the lost years, today Justin needs you."

"I'm a stranger, Annie," he said grimly. "But this isn't about my mistakes or yours. It's about Justin." He swallowed, gaze blazing into hers with a fire that spoke of his feelings. "It's about helping our son. What he needs is truth. And he's going to get it."

She didn't agree that Sloan was a stranger, but she wasn't going to argue the matter. He and Justin had a natural bond. It was visible when they worked in the garden or played catch or joked with each other in a male way that made no sense to

Annie but had them both grinning. Something inside Justin had instinctively gravitated toward his biological father. She'd been afraid at first, but now she'd begun to believe Sloan Hawkins was exactly what her child needed.

As scared as she was of Justin's reaction, she asked, "Will you come over tonight? I'll have Delaney spend the night with my parents so we can talk to him freely."

"I'll be there."

He squeezed her hand and went inside the house.

Sloan's insides felt as raw as hamburger meat. If a man could get a bleeding ulcer in one day, he'd gotten one. For those few minutes sitting beside Annie on the Hawkins's veranda, looking out over the gardens as they'd done as teens, he'd felt…right, somehow. And he'd felt like a father worrying over his son.

He'd known the moment he walked inside this house and seen Annie Crawford again that he wouldn't leave unscathed. But he'd never imagined the tangled mess he'd discover—worse than the tangle of vines and weeds in the Wedding Garden.

Where did a man begin to make up for years of absence? Would Justin even want an unknown father in his life? Perhaps the better question was would Annie allow it? She needed him now as moral support, but what about afterward?

He slammed a fist into his palm.

Who was he kidding? He couldn't be a father even if Annie and Justin allowed it. Considering his home and business were in Virginia, he'd leave again someday. He'd never belonged in Redemption and still didn't want to be here.

No, that wasn't entirely true.

But true enough.

Like a prizefighter shadowboxing, he was jabbing himself to pieces with indecision and uncertainty.

Frustrated, confused and antsy for the meeting tonight, he worked in the garden until Annie left for the day. Then he went inside, showered and headed for Aunt Lydia's room. She'd only been awake once today when he'd popped in.

This time her eyes were open. "Sloanie."

The boyhood endearment was barely a whisper.

"Auntie," he said, going to sit beside her. "What's my best girl need?"

The false cheer wasn't lost on her.

She lifted a weak hand and he covered the smooth skin with his. His sunshine tan against her indoor pallor saddened him. He didn't know how he was going to handle losing this woman. She had been his anchor when the whole world had collapsed around him.

"I need my boy to find happiness."

"I'm happy as a lark. Got a great life. A great business. The best aunt in the world."

"Sloanie," she said again, the soft word a rebuke. He'd never been able to fool her. "I don't have much time left. I love you so much. I don't want you to be sad or angry when I go."

He bent to kiss her cheek, the knot in his chest tightening. He didn't want to talk about this. "I love you, too."

"I have to tell you some things." Her voice was weak and raspy with breathlessness.

"Don't tire yourself out. We can talk anytime."

"No, honey. Time is short. I must talk now."

"Don't." The word choked him.

She slid her hand from beneath his to pat his arm. She'd always comforted him this way.

"Sloanie, I'm not afraid of dying. I'm ready. Eager at times, but I don't want to leave you alone and searching. You've searched your entire life for one thing or another."

And never found anything.

Sloan wanted to fall against his beloved aunt and weep as he'd done as a child, but his distress would only worry her more, so he remained still. "Don't worry about me. Take care of you. I want you well."

"I will be well soon, but not in the way you want. Heaven has no heart disease, no sorrow or regret."

The knot in his chest became a boulder. "Heaven should welcome you with open arms. You're the most perfect person I've ever known."

"We don't get to Heaven on *our* perfection. We get there on *His*. Remember that, baby. You can't be bad enough or good enough. Just let go and let God take over. I've made my share of mistakes. Your daddy. Your mama. Ulysses. Yet Jesus forgave and loved me anyway."

He stroked her soft fingers calmly, but his belly jittered. His parents were not his favorite topics. And Popbottle Jones? He had no idea where to go with that. "You didn't make their choices for them."

His father had chosen to commit murder. His mother had chosen to leave behind a scared child in exchange for a man.

"No, but I spoiled my brother. Clayton was a late in life baby. I was nearly grown. He thought the world revolved around him. When he went to prison, I should have taken in you and your mama. But she was a proud woman and I was angry, blaming her for Clayton's downfall."

"You took me."

"Yes." She patted again, radiating the light of love. "You were the joy God sent. *He* filled the emptiness in my spirit, but *you* filled the emptiness in my heart."

His eyes began to burn. "I was no prize."

"Yes, you were. But life hurt you and I couldn't fix it."

He couldn't argue with that. "I'm a big boy now."

"Yet you never wanted to come home. You never wanted

to face your pain or your past. You still carry those old wounds." Her breath was short and Sloan wanted to make her stop, but she seemed determined to talk—as though she was running out of time. "God can set you free, my darling boy. He can heal your wounds. I can't leave without telling you. Promise me you'll give Him a chance. He's such a good Father." Her frail hand gripped his arm with surprising strength. "Promise me."

What else could he say? Heart breaking, fighting tears, he nodded.

"I promise."

Sloan parked his bike in the driveway next to Annie's car and approached the concrete porch. Her house was a modest frame with a tidy yard, but from the looks of things, the rest could use some attention. A fascia board was loose on the porch overhang where red wasps had built a nest. He dodged one of the ever-angry insects and kept an eye on another.

The house needed a coat of paint, too. He still didn't understand why Annie wouldn't accept his money. He had plenty with no one to spend it on except Lydia. Justin was his child and except for a baseball glove and a six-pack of Gatorade, he'd never contributed a penny to his care. From the looks of things, Annie could use the help. Maybe he'd try to talk to her about it again. Money was something he could provide even after he went back to Virginia.

He pressed the doorbell and then noticed the neatly printed note taped below it. "Knock. Doorbell broken."

He knocked, more determined to have that little financial chat. But not tonight.

The knot in his gut turned to rock. Life seemed to be moving too fast since his return to Redemption. He'd come home to be with a dying relative and discovered a new, even more fragile relative waiting—his son. He could do nothing for Lydia, a fact that ripped him in half. He hoped he could do more for Justin.

After the heart-wrenching conversation, he'd asked a neighbor to sit with his aunt until he returned. The small boy hiding inside prayed she would still be there. Without her, he lost his roots and his life had no anchor.

He lifted a fist to knock again just as the door swung open.

Annie had changed from scrubs into denim cropped pants and a tank top. With her Cameron Diaz cheeks flushed and her hair whipped up into a ponytail, she looked eighteen again.

Sloan's pulse kicked into overdrive. Unsettled, he motioned to a low-flying wasp. "Look out. Dive-bomber at three o'clock."

"I despise those things. Delaney got stung yesterday."

"Is she okay?"

"After the initial screaming, yes. The place is red and hot, but she's not allergic. Thank God." She pushed the door back with the flat of her hand and stood aside to let him enter. "I'm so nervous, I'm sick to my stomach."

"About a wasp?" He knew she referred to Justin, but was trying to tease her into relaxing. He was nervous enough himself, but Annie needed his strength and calm, not his anxiety. He hadn't been around when she'd needed him before and he wasn't going to let her down this time.

She gave him a look. "No, knothead. About the cake I'm baking for the church dinner."

He laughed and to his pleasure, so did she. Sloan hooked an arm over her shoulders. She'd always been more than a match for his smart mouth. "That's my girl."

As soon as he said the words, Annie stiffened and slid away. He sighed. She wasn't his girl. She'd made that as clear as a baby's conscience.

Following her into the neat living room, he asked, "Where's Justin?"

"In his room. I'll get him. Sit down." But before she left the room, Justin came sauntering in.

His face registered curiosity. "Hi, Sloan. What's up?"

Sloan's adrenaline kicked in, as jolting as six cups of coffee. This was his son. The wonder and power of that revelation rocked his world.

"Justin." The two exchanged knuckle bumps. "Your mother and I want to talk to you."

Annie sucked in a noisy breath. Her green eyes shot him a look of panic.

"No time like the present," he told her quietly and with all the reassurance he could.

"I don't know— I just thought." She looked from the now-bewildered boy to him. "Do you want some cookies? Or maybe something to drink first?"

"Later." Sloan settled on the beige microfiber couch, trying with all his might to appear calmer than he felt. "Sit down, Justin. Annie, you, too. You're flitting around more than those red wasps."

With another nervous exhale, Annie perched, pulling Justin down beside her. She'd maneuvered the boy so that Sloan was on one side and she on the other. Sloan itched to hold and comfort her, to relieve her stress and promise that everything would be all right. He would *make* it all right. Somehow.

"What's going on, Mom?" Justin asked, his voice sounding young and unsure.

Annie gripped one of the boy's hands between both of hers. "We—that is, Sloan and I—"

Justin frowned. "Yeah?"

"You know how much I love you, don't you, baby?"

The boy shot a glance at Sloan. When Sloan offered a reassuring nod, a light came on in Justin's face.

"This is about what I asked you, isn't it?" His question was for Sloan. "About what Robbie said?"

"Yes, and I made you a promise." Sloan scooted closer, his knee bumping Justin's. "I'm not sure what you heard, so your mother and I want you to know the truth from us."

"So, are you or not?"

Blood pounding in his temples, Sloan exchanged glances with Annie and then spoke the words he knew would change his life and that of this child. "Yes. I'm your biological father."

Sloan wasn't sure what he expected from the boy, but Justin took the news calmly, though his throat worked and his eyes gleamed suspiciously. "So, where have you been? Why didn't you marry my mom?"

Annie spoke up, her voice gentle. "He didn't know about you."

Justin's head snapped toward his mother. "Why not?"

"The answer to that is complicated," she went on. "Something bad happened and Sloan left town before I could tell him."

Justin's sharp mind would not leave the vagaries alone. "What kind of bad thing? Why did you leave my mom?"

Well, lovely, Sloan thought sarcastically. He'd opened this can of worms and now he had to eat it. "I was accused of a crime I didn't commit. I had a choice to leave town or go to jail."

"And you ran?" Justin's opinion of that was clear.

"If I had known about you I would have stayed and fought. And I would have married your mom," Sloan said, holding the boy's gaze with his. "I told you I loved her. And I meant it. I would have done anything for her. *Anything.*"

Annie would never know, but *she* was the reason he'd run, not the criminal accusation. He'd left town to save her, not knowing his departure would only cause her more trouble.

He heard the soft intake of Annie's breath and ventured a glance at her face. Flushed, eyes glassy, soft mouth parted in surprise, she stared at him. He knew she wanted to ask why he hadn't told her everything that night, but she wouldn't ask now in front of Justin. Tonight was for the boy.

"Is that why Grandpa doesn't like you? Does he know about me?"

"Your Grandpa never liked me, Justin. You had nothing to do with that."

"Grandpa doesn't know. Only your dad—" Annie caught herself "—only Joey knew for sure."

"So, that's why he hated me."

"Oh, Justin." Annie's words were despairing.

Sloan's fists were tight against his thighs. He ached from the knowledge that his son had lived his whole life believing he was not loved by his father. "Joey thought he was doing the right thing, Justin. He took care of you and your mother. We have to give him credit for that."

But Justin wasn't ready to cut Joey any slack. "Why doesn't he like Delaney? She's not like me. She's a good kid."

All right, that was enough. Sloan put a firm hand on Justin's knee. Lydia's words, spoken long ago, came out of his mouth. "You listen to me. None of this is your fault. You're a good boy. Everyone goes through rough times but that doesn't make you bad."

Annie circled an arm around her son's waist. "He's right, baby. You're a wonderful son and I wouldn't trade you for anyone else."

"Even when I do stupid stuff?"

Annie grinned. "Even then. But that doesn't mean I want you to do any more of it."

Justin allowed a grin, too. "Yeah, I figured that."

Sloan breathed a sigh of relief. This had gone better than either he or Annie had expected. Brushing a hand down his clean jeans, he rose. "I want you to know something, Justin."

"What? You expect me to be out slaving over a delphinium first thing in the morning?"

"Yeah, that, too." Sloan laughed and was sorely tempted to hug the kid. Sometimes a wisecrack came in handy. "You're a real help to me. I couldn't accomplish near as much without you. But that's not the most important thing. I haven't been here for you. I regret that more than I can tell you, and I hope, long after the garden is finished, you'll let me be part of your life."

The speech was longer than he'd intended to give, but the words needed saying.

Justin pulled away from his mother and rose, too, coming up to Sloan's shoulder. One of these days, the boy would be as tall as he was. The thought gave him a hitch beneath his ribcage. This was his child, his baby, his son.

Before he could stop himself, Sloan pulled Justin against his chest and thumped his back once. The boy came willingly, all bones and sinews and smelling of pizza. Sloan breathed him in, a feeling of regret and joy so profound washing through him that he couldn't have spoken if he'd tried.

He thumped his son's back one more time and stepped away.

Justin stood before him, lanky arms dangling at his sides, half little boy, half adolescent. And his next words rocked Sloan's world.

"Does this mean you and Mom are getting married now?"

Chapter Eight

Annie was emotionally drained.

Long after Justin's stunning question that had turned her face to fire and shocked Sloan to temporary silence, the two adults had talked and listened. But mostly they'd danced around the volatile, impossible question. At eleven, Justin should understand that relationships were not as simple as he wanted them to be.

"Do you want any more coffee?" she asked Sloan. They'd adjourned to the kitchen two hours ago when Sloan, in a clear attempt to move past their son's query, had challenged Justin and her to a game of Uno. Finally, after another hour, Justin had wound down enough to go to bed. Since then she and Sloan had shared coffee and conversation, most of it as serious as the night's events.

He put a hand over his coffee cup. "I'll be up until dawn as it is."

She snorted. "No kidding. But your ploy with the Uno game was brilliant."

"It was the only thing I could think of to channel his mind in a new direction."

"Otherwise, he would have been up all night, too." And he might have pushed the marriage issue, a question that had put crazy thoughts in Annie's head.

She carried the dirty coffee mugs to the sink. When she turned, Sloan was behind her with the cream and sugar set.

"Where do these go?"

"Up there." She opened a cabinet door. "I'm still amazed that you convinced him to get some sleep."

"The threat of sweating in the sun without any sleep is a powerful motivator."

As he reached over her head, he bumped her side with his. Annie knew she should step away from the contact, however incidental, but she didn't. Having Sloan near felt better than it should. "So are the twenty extra dollars you promised him."

He chuckled. "True. I am an astute businessman. And so, apparently, is my son."

Annie turned the faucet in the sink, the spray adding backdrop to their conversation. "How do you feel about all this, Sloan? You have to be stunned."

He stood so close she could feel the heat of his body and could see the tiny pulse beat over his temple. He smelled of coffee and spice and of the fresh outdoors. If anything, Sloan Hawkins was more attractive today than he'd ever been, and not just physically, though there was definitely that.

He looked down at her, one hand braced on the countertop, face serious. "I'm still processing."

Whatever that meant. Scared she was setting herself up for more hurt, Annie edged a step away.

"The important thing," he said, filling the space she'd just vacated, "is that Justin seems to be okay."

"Telling him was easier than I expected. I was relieved to get the truth out in the open."

"Where do we go from here?"

Drying her hands on a towel, Annie turned and leaned her hips against the counter edge, thoughtful. "I'm not sure what you mean."

"Justin. Me. You."

"I don't know." Carefully, she folded the tea towel, unsure of what he wanted her to say and even more uncertain of what she wanted. "I think he needs you in his life, especially now when the information is new and startling. It would be wrong to dump this on him and then walk away." Which was exactly what she expected Sloan to do.

Sloan's jaw worked. "I won't."

"I hope you mean that. I can't bear to see him hurt anymore."

"He's my son. I want to know him."

"How is that going to be possible?"

"He can come to Virginia."

Annie's heart dropped. "No."

"Why not? D.C. is a few minutes away from my offices. I can take him lots of cool places he's never seen."

"I don't know. It's scary to think of him so far away."

"You don't trust me with him." The statement was said with an edge of bitterness.

"I—" Maybe he was right. But what did he expect? "I can't pretend the past didn't happen."

Sloan's shoulders slumped for a second and then he stepped away from the counter and from her, expression hard. "That's what I figured. But let's get one thing straight. I'm going to be in his life, whether you trust me or not."

And with that unsettling threat dangling in the air like a noose, he walked out of her house, fired up his Harley and roared away.

Sloan lay on his boyhood bed, still fully dressed—except for his boots, of course. Lydia would thump his head for putting dirty feet on her hand-stitched quilt.

Lydia. He rubbed at his grainy eyes, sorrow pressing against them with such power that he required all his will not to cry like a big baby. The neighbor had graciously stayed at his aunt's side while he was visiting Annie and Justin, although Sloan had called several times and offered to rush home. Lydia, the neighbor said, only awakened once.

He sighed, his chest almost too heavy to lift. Tonight he'd made another mess. Though the conversation with Justin had gone well, Sloan's smart mouth had managed to alienate Annie again.

She'd stabbed him through the heart with her distrust. Rationally, he knew she had reason, or at least she believed she did. He knew better, and that knowledge was starting to eat on him. He'd almost told her the entire story, but Annie loved her father and believed the best of him. If she knew what Dooley had done, she'd be devastated. Why break up a family just because he didn't have one?

Justin's face floated into his consciousness. He did have a family. Sort of. He'd never given fatherhood much thought, but now that he knew about Justin, he wanted him. The weird thing was he wanted the sunshiny little girl, Delaney, too.

With a groan, he threw an arm over his eyes. "Annie."

He'd *always* wanted Annie. All of this was her fault. He loved her kids because they were part of her, and he loved her.

"God, I don't know what to do."

God.

His conversation with Lydia came tumbling in. He'd promised to give some thought to God.

No time like the present. He wasn't sleeping anyway. Although he wasn't sure of the protocol for ringing up God in the middle of the night, he remembered boyhood prayers.

He threw his legs over the side of the bed, his feet touching down on a soft throw rug—the same rug he'd knelt on as a heartbroken boy, begging God to bring his mother back.

"Where were You, God?" he asked. "Lydia says You're there. Annie, too. Where are You?"

He felt a little stupid talking out loud to the darkness, but he did anyway. He'd always believed in God. He just figured God didn't believe in him all that much. Aunt Lydia said he was wrong, and he believed her now in a way he hadn't when he was young and stupid. His aunt was a wise lady.

He'd considered the time twelve years ago to be the lowest point in his life. Confused, tormented, ostracized from everything and everyone he'd loved, he'd been too young, foolish and angry to cry out to God.

Tonight he was an adult with enough wisdom to know he could no longer do this by himself. Even though he'd built a successful business and had plenty of money, life still felt empty. *He* felt empty. A million dollars couldn't buy happiness or peace of mind or love. And those were things he lacked.

"All right, God, just me and You talking. Okay?" And he began to pray.

Streaks of dawn, pink and pretty, crept into the upstairs bedroom and awakened Sloan from what had to be a very short nap.

He was on his knees, next to the bed, his face smashed against the smooth old quilt. Sitting back, he discovered his foot was asleep and gingerly stretched his legs on the rug.

As awareness came to him, he remembered the last twenty-four hours. Though his eyes were gritty and his head groggy, he felt renewed and refreshed, not on the outside, but inside. A quiet assurance filled the space that had once churned with turmoil.

Something had happened to him. Something he could not explain, but in that time of talking to God, a light had gone on inside his head. He figured people would say that Hawkins boy had finally gone off the deep end if he told anyone, but he had come into this room last night alone and this morning a Presence was with him.

Emotion clogged his throat. God had heard and answered. He'd heard no angels singing, but he figured they were. Or maybe they were shocked silent.

He grinned at the thought.

Who would figure a security expert with a knack for knocking heads would find God?

"Thanks, Lord," he said. The feeling had returned to his legs, so he slipped on his boots. Normally, he set his alarm to check on Lydia every couple of hours anyway. When she awoke this morning, he'd have good news to share.

Quietly, he descended the stairs, peeked in to find her sleeping as he'd expected, and went into the kitchen to start coffee. Last night, he'd overindulged in caffeine at Annie's, but this morning, he could use the jump start.

While the smell was filling the room, he set out the ingredients for pancakes. Annie and the kids would be here at seven. Generally, she fed Lydia and the kids before her mother picked up Delaney for the day and Justin went to work in the gardens with him.

Humming, he cracked the eggs against the bowl and added them to the flour and sugar and his special secret ingredients—melted butter, buttermilk and a touch of vanilla. Annie would be surprised to discover pancakes cooking when she arrived.

He smiled to himself. She'd be a lot more surprised when he shared his news.

Annie arrived to the smell of fried bacon and fresh coffee.

"I'm impressed," she said, setting her purse and nurse's bag aside. "The man cooks." *And looks really good in the process.*

"This smells awesome," Delaney added, batting long black

eyelashes at Sloan. She was already full of smiles and energy even this early in the morning.

"Beats cold cereal." Sloan was at the counter next to the stove, dipping pancake batter into a black cast-iron skillet. "Grab a plate. Or better yet, set the table for us, Delaney, and Justin, you pour juice or milk. Whatever you want."

Justin, who'd been even quieter than usual this morning, did as Sloan asked without comment. Sloan cocked an eyebrow at Annie. All she could do was shrug. After Sloan left last night, she'd spent an hour or more thinking and praying for their child to be all right. But, like his father, Justin was hard to read. He could be thrilled or devastated and she'd never know unless he exploded.

"You appear to have things under control here," she said. "I'll go check on Miss Lydia."

One hand on the skillet handle and the other wielding a spatula, Sloan glanced over a shoulder. "She was still asleep when I came down. I have something important to tell her so let me know if she's awake."

Annie assumed he meant Justin. So did Justin, because the child whipped around from the fridge, juice bottle in hand.

Sloan hitched his chin toward the wide-eyed boy. "We'll talk about that later. Your opinion counts."

Justin gave a short nod and carried the juice to the table. Bewildered, Annie realized the two males had just agreed to something she didn't understand but that had satisfied them both. Was this the way it was supposed to be between a father and a son?

Chewing on the interesting thought, she traversed the hall to Lydia's room and went inside.

"Good morning, Miss Lydia." She stepped to the bed and placed a hand on her patient's shoulder, going through the morning assessment routine. Lydia's color was more cyanotic today, her respirations more shallow.

The dear lady didn't move. Annie gently shook her. "Lydia."

Tired eyes opened. Bluish lips barely curved. "Hi, honey."

Annie smiled, but the nurse inside was frowning. "Let's check your blood pressure."

For once, Lydia didn't protest. Annie checked her pressure and listened to her heart and lungs with a stethoscope. Though the results were not good, Annie maintained a professional demeanor. She'd been preparing for this time, praying about it, steadying her own emotions. Lydia needed her friendship and her medical expertise, not her tears. So would Sloan.

"Where's Sloan?" Lydia murmured.

"Making pancakes for the kids and waiting for you to wake up."

"Like a family," the older lady whispered, expression soft.

With a jolt, Annie realized it was true. Worse, she liked the idea too much.

"He has something important to tell you."

"Justin?"

"I'm not sure, but Sloan and I told Justin last night, and the conversation went well, I think." Leaving the blood-pressure cuff in place, Annie jotted the reading and time in a folder she kept at the bedside.

"Truth will set you free."

"Yes," she agreed, though her mind was not on the conversation. "Your blood pressure is too low this morning. Will you change your mind about the hospital?" Lydia had created a living will indicating her wish to die at home. The time was fast approaching.

"I'm not afraid. This is where I belong."

Annie knew the answer before Lydia spoke, but in good conscience, she'd had to ask.

"Do you need anything? Want anything?"

"Sloan."

"I'll get him."

Heavy-hearted, Annie went into the kitchen. The kids and Sloan were chowing down. "Your aunt wants you."

Bad news must have shown on her face, because he took one look, rose from the table and left the room.

"Finish your breakfast, kids," Annie said, her eyes following Sloan's journey down the hall. "I'm calling Grandma to come get both of you."

Around a mouthful of pancake, Justin protested. "But Sloan and I are working—"

"Not today, son. Miss Lydia isn't doing well." She reached for the phone and punched in the numbers.

Justin swallowed. "Is she gonna die?"

"No one knows for sure, but the signs are there."

Both children grew silent. Interest in Sloan's pancakes went out the window. The kids, like so many others, including herself, cared for Miss Lydia. And though Annie had talked to them repeatedly about the lady's health, losing Lydia would be hard on everyone—especially Sloan.

After a quick phone call to her mother and another to Lydia's physician, Annie went to be with her patient. This was the part of being a hospice nurse that she'd trained for, one of the reasons she'd chosen this job. She wanted to be a help to a patient and family in this hardest of times. But she'd never been this close to a patient before. Or to the patient's only family.

When she reentered the room, Sloan was seated at the bedside, holding Lydia's pale hand between his dark ones. A tight fist of emotion squeezed Annie's heart.

"God changed me, Lydia. I'm a new man. You were right, and now I wonder why I waited so long."

So that was why Sloan seemed different this morning.

Stunned and thrilled, Annie paused in the doorway, unsure

about listening in on such a personal conversation, but needing to be with her patient. And if she'd admit it, she wanted to be near Sloan, too.

Lydia's gaze flickered toward her. The chair groaned slightly as Sloan twisted. "You heard?"

"I did. And I think it's wonderful."

He smiled. "Yeah. Pretty sweet."

Lydia's eyes glowed with happiness. Her mouth barely moved. "I am proud…of you. Good man. My boy."

Her chest rose and fell, the breathing labored. Annie stepped up next to Sloan and placed her fingers on Lydia's limp wrist. She could feel Sloan's worry, but he was handling himself well. Instinctively, he'd given his dying aunt the one thing she wanted most.

"You should rest now, Lydia. You're exhausting yourself."

Lydia's smile was tender. "Take care…of each other."

Annie placed her other hand on Sloan's shoulder. He had to know his aunt was saying goodbye. "We'll be fine." What else could she say?

"Promise?"

Sloan had gone still and his shoulders were tense beneath her touch. If he hadn't known before, he understood now.

"I'll promise you anything," he said, voice husky with emotion. "Anything. Next summer we'll go to Rome."

But Lydia was past listening. "Hold on to…Jesus."

Annie's vision blurred. She blinked hard.

Sloan gripped Lydia's hand as though his powerful life force could keep her here. "I will."

As if waiting to hear those words, Lydia smiled and closed her eyes.

"The garden will be done soon." There was desperation in Sloan's voice. "We'll have weddings there again. We'll go to Rome and Egypt and anywhere else you want to go."

But Lydia didn't respond. The pale blue eyes never opened again. Her chest rose one last time and then went still.

Annie placed her stethoscope over the valiant heart and listened.

"Sloan," she said softly as she removed the instrument, the clack of earpieces the only sound. "She's gone."

"No, she's not gone. She can't be." He continued to hold the limp hand, rubbing his thumbs over the pale, blue-veined skin again and again. "Lydia. Auntie." His voice cracked. "I love you."

Annie thought her heart would rip right out of her chest. "She knew, Sloan. She always knew."

He put his head down on the edge of the bed. Voice muffled, he said, "Don't die. God, please, don't take her. I need her. I can't—"

Aching to comfort him, Annie touched his shoulder again. This time she stroked one hand along the soft cotton of his T-shirt. "Let her go, Sloan. This is what she wanted. Her body was tired. Look how beautiful she is now. No longer struggling to breathe, no longer weak and exhausted. Look at her, Sloan." For indeed, Lydia glowed with peace, her ever-present smile even more gentle and confident in death than in life.

With soul-wrenching tenderness, Sloan rose, kissed his aunt's pale cheek and whispered something against her snowy hair. Then, looking like the lost soul he'd always been, he turned to Annie. "I don't know what to do."

He seemed so alone. Everything in her wanted to hold him. "The rest is my job, Sloan. But would you mind calling Mr. Jones? I don't want him to hear it on the grapevine."

"Right. Sure."

As he left the room, head down and tread heavy, Annie let the tears come—for Lydia, for herself, but most of all for Sloan.

* * *

Word of Lydia's death spread like a virus and by noon, a constant string of visitors began coming with casseroles, cakes and condolences. Sloan knew they came because of their love for Lydia, not for him, but he appreciated the gestures anyway. Lydia deserved their honor.

Late that afternoon, he made the painful trek to the funeral home, grateful when Annie came along. He hadn't asked and she hadn't offered. She'd simply slipped her hand in his and come.

God, he loved her.

God again. Sloan wanted to be angry at God, but he wasn't. Lydia wouldn't want that. If he'd ever needed God, he needed Him now.

Later, back at the house, he went through the motions, greeted neighbors, tasted blackberry cobbler and fresh corn and sliced tomatoes. By sundown, he was too emotionally drained to continue. With Annie quietly handling the visitors, all of whom she knew better than he did, he'd slipped out the French doors into the garden.

A sharp pang of regret pierced him. He'd badly wanted Lydia to see the Wedding Garden restored to its former glory. The rose arbor was in place and for that he was glad. She'd been able to see the blooms from her window and she'd loved them. But there was much more left to do. He'd dreamed of restoring the entire acre and taking her for a stroll down meandering paths, past the fountain, through the perennials, to the sitting area he and Mrs. Miller had planned for the shade beneath the red maples. Lydia would have been pleased.

He had already ordered the benches and thousands of bedding plants. If he finished the work, would she know somehow?

He roamed from one end of the vast space to the other, past the completed work and into the area where a spray of three fountains had once shot from the ground but where weeds and unwanted plants now encroached. He'd have to order more mulch.

The dying sun cast rays of orange and gold across the open spaces, sliced through the maples and gilded the plants.

Dozens of couples—maybe hundreds—had exchanged wedding vows in this place over the years. His grandparents and parents had married here. During the weeks since his arrival, he'd encountered any number of townspeople excited about the restoration because they or someone in their family had married or attended parties in the Hawkins's garden. He hadn't cared about that before, but now he did.

Rudderless without Aunt Lydia, this house and garden and its heritage were all the roots he had left.

Though he'd donned dress slacks and shiny black shoes out of respect for his aunt, Sloan went to his knees and began to tear at the weeds with his hands. Lydia had wanted the Wedding Garden to be a place for creating beautiful memories again, and even if she was gone, Sloan could grant her wish.

Restoring the garden before his return to Virginia would be his final tribute to Lydia's memory.

He began tugging at the thick weeds, tossing them aside as he ripped them from the ground. Without gloves his hands stung and dirt embedded beneath his nails, but he yanked and pulled and tossed. The sun disappeared and dusk moved in on stealthy feet.

He worked on, more by feel as darkness overtook him and only the light from the veranda illuminated the space. Envisioning romantic night strolls in the garden, he planned to place solar lamps along the path and around the fountain, the benches and as edging along the picket fence. But those were in the future.

He heard the French doors open and click shut again. Then

soft footfalls caught his ear. He sat back on his heels, grimly satisfied at the weedy carnage spread over the ground.

He didn't bother to turn around. He knew who was coming. Annie. His heart could recognize her in a dark room filled with hundreds of people.

"Sloan," she called softly. "Where are you?"

"Here." He rose and the movement must have been enough for she came directly to him.

"Are you all right?"

"Sure." *No.*

"Everyone's gone."

"I didn't mean to run out on you." But he'd not been able to bear one more kind word without breaking down.

He stretched his back, surprised at the stiffness. He'd been out here longer than he'd thought.

"You needed some time."

He drew in a deep draft of green-scented air, held the breath as long as he could then released it in a rush. "I can't believe she's gone."

"Neither can I. She's been part of my life for as long as I can remember. In this last year of caring for her…" Annie's voice trailed off. She was hurting, too.

He could handle his own grief. Knowing Annie hurt was a different matter. Sloan hooked an arm over her shoulders and snugged her close to his side. "She loved you like a daughter."

"I know." Annie sniffed and turned her face into his chest. With a sigh, almost of relief, she slid both arms around his waist and rested against him.

"My hands are dirty," he said, but held her anyway.

"Doesn't matter. I just need to hold you. I wanted to earlier, but—" Her words were a balm to his bleeding soul. "If losing Lydia tears me up, I can only imagine how you are feeling."

Sloan took another deep, sighing breath and drew in the

scent of Annie's hair mingled with fresh earth and new blossoms. The feel of her, the smell of her, the essence of who she was and what she'd always been filled him. He absorbed her strength and kindness, grateful to her in more ways than he could ever express—and loved her more than he ever had.

"Annie," he whispered, holding her tighter than he should have, desperate for the comfort she offered.

She raised her head to look at him and the moonlight turned her skin to gold. When she touched his cheek, he trembled, the pain he'd held inside all day—maybe all his life—welling in his eyes.

"Sloanie," she murmured, and tiptoed up to place a sweet, gentle, comforting kiss against the corner of his mouth.

And Sloan was forever lost.

Chapter Nine

The day of the funeral, Annie fussed with her hair and fretted, unable to get the kiss out of her mind. She didn't know what had come over her in the garden that night. When tears had glistened in Sloan's eyes, she'd thought only to comfort him. Yet as soon as her lips touched his skin, she'd known the kiss was a mistake. She'd meant the gesture as kindness, but her foolish heart didn't understand.

He'd tasted like Sloan. A little salty, a lot dangerous, and all man.

She shivered at the too-pleasant memory. One look in the mirror told her she was blushing. She patted the high cheekbones with translucent powder to cover the reaction. She was too mature and had been through too much to behave like a teenager mooning over the town bad boy.

But thoughts of Sloan wouldn't leave her alone. He'd tilted his face ever so slightly and caught her lips full-on, returning the kiss—a brief, sorrowful joining. Then they'd simply stood there, surrounded by fireflies and roses and croaking tree frogs, holding one another. Her emotions had been too jumbled to speak.

Shared grief and the basic human need for comfort had morphed into something she was unprepared for.

Annie was very much afraid that she was falling in love with him again. Maybe she'd never stopped.

A tight knot filled her throat.

She slid a dangling pearl into one earlobe.

Since Lydia's death, Sloan had been on the telephone and the computer more than ever, doing business, talking to friends in Virginia, sure signs that Redemption was still the last place on earth he wanted to be.

She didn't know what she wanted from Sloan Hawkins, but one thing was for certain: she wasn't ready for him to leave.

Lydia's funeral was magnificent.

The line of people signing the guest book grew longer and longer as the church filled to the brim. The funeral director, Tim Chaney, brought in folding chairs for the overflow. Like everyone else in town, he'd known Lydia all his life.

"Every summer when I was a kid, Miss Lydia bought lemonade from my stand," he told Sloan. "She said I made the best in the world." He chuckled softly. "She had to know I used a packaged mix, but I felt like a real entrepreneur when she said it."

Tim's was one of a dozen such stories Sloan had heard in the last three days. Aunt Lydia made people feel special.

He shook the man's hand. "Thanks, Tim."

The woman at Sloan's side took his elbow. Dressed in a sleek black dress with her red hair curving on her shoulders, classy Tara Brighton didn't look like one of the best bodyguards in the business, but she was, and Sloan was her employer. Tara was one of three friends who had flown in from Virginia and now surrounded him with their support. He appreciated the trio, but the only people he really wanted had yet to arrive.

He'd asked Annie and the children to ride with him in the family car. She'd declined. The refusal bothered him. Justin was family whether Annie liked it or not, though no one else shared that information. Sloan figured Annie was afraid of speculation, especially from her father. The chief was already giving her fits about spending time at the Hawkins's place now that Lydia was gone. In his eyes, and in Sloan's, Annie deserved better than that Hawkins boy.

Sloan straightened his tie one more time, acid gnawing his belly. He dreaded the moment he had to walk into the sanctuary and see Aunt Lydia's casket.

Flanked by Tara and Max Jett, the intelligence specialist, with the dangerous-looking bruiser Harrison pulling rear guard, Sloan entered the church from a side door and took his place on the front pew. Even with these trusted employees, he felt alone. He and Lydia were the last of a dying breed of Hawkinses.

But he hadn't felt alone that night in the garden. With Annie in his arms, he'd been whole again.

He tried to shut out the memory, but it lingered and tapped at the back of his brain. He'd stepped over the line that night, kissing Annie when all she'd wanted to do was offer condolences. Neither had spoken of it since, but the incident hovered between them. The bad thing was if given the choice, he'd kiss her again in a heartbeat. So much for wanting the best for her.

He shifted on the padded pew, wishing he'd requested happier music. Mingled with his thoughts of Annie and Justin and losing Lydia, the unnaturally hushed sounds of recorded music depressed him. Lydia would have liked a celebration, not a dirge.

Murmurs rippled around him and he figured speculation was already circulating about his friends, particularly the beautiful Tara. Redemption gossips likely pegged her as a girlfriend. Sloan figured it was none of their business, but didn't feel quite as adamant about the sentiment as he had a couple of months ago. Prayer was smoothing the sharp edges from his anger. Prayer and long talks with Annie.

His gut tightened. Annie again.

When someone clapped a hand on his shoulder, Sloan seized the opportunity to search for Annie and the kids. He turned to exchange handshakes with Jace Carter, the quiet carpenter who'd done repairs on Lydia's veranda and built a wheelchair ramp. Sloan liked the guy and wouldn't mind knowing him better.

"Thanks for coming," he murmured, but couldn't keep from gazing beyond Jace. He saw Annie's father and mother, the Bowmans, the Martinellis from the Sugar Shack, and a host of other familiar faces, but no Annie. Disappointed, he turned his attentions to the front and the inevitable service.

Jace murmured in his ear. "She's coming in now."

The knowledge shot a bolt of energy through Sloan's exhausted body. He didn't care what anyone thought. He looked around and his eyes met Annie's. He must have looked as stricken as he felt, because she offered a serene smile of encouragement and a quick narrowing of green eyes.

He wanted her here, next to him. Annie had been Lydia's friend and nurse. The town knew that and should accept her rightful place among the mourners. Shouldn't they?

Throwing caution to the wind, he hitched his chin, hoping she understood his silent plea. She spoke something to Justin and then gripped Delaney's hand and started down the aisle toward him and the half-empty pew. Sloan's belly leaped.

When his employees parted to make room for the newcomers, the murmurs of speculation intensified. Annie took the place to his left, bringing with her a clean, vanilla scent that was a comfort in itself. Gorgeous in a simple jade dress, she gripped a small white handbag in her lap.

"How are you?" she whispered.

"Overwhelmed."

She nodded and he knew she understood. Lydia's death following on the heels of the revelation about Justin was too much to process at one time.

Instead of sitting by her mother as Justin did, the irrepressible Delaney wiggled onto the pew between Sloan and Tara. She looked cute in a sunflower dress and shiny white shoes with her blond hair curling softly on her shoulders. He winked at her. With a sweet smile, she slipped her hand into one of his. That tiny action held a wealth of compassion. Delaney started to say something but a rustle of movement up front indicated the service was about to start.

The dread returned like a boulder in his gut. And Sloan turned his attention to the inevitable.

Over the next painfully long thirty minutes, Sloan's mind wandered in and out with memories of the aunt who had loved him when no one else would. Scrapes and bruises, blackened eyes and bad attitude, juvenile hall and young love. Lydia hadn't backed away from any of it, though he had never been an easy child.

He heard snatches of Pastor Parker's message, bits and pieces of Lydia's favorite songs sung by church members who sniffed and dabbed at red eyes as they sang. When Ulysses E. Jones stepped up to the microphone with the eulogy, Sloan tried to focus. Each time he glanced at the white casket draped with pink roses, his mind went blank again.

She couldn't be gone. She just couldn't. But she was.

"Lydia Margaret Hawkins was my friend," Popbottle Jones began.

Asking the old professor to bring the eulogy was a no-brainer. Though Sloan didn't know the whole story, he was sure there was more between his aunt and the dignified

Dumpster diver. Sloan hadn't cared if Popbottle wore his usual mismatched cast-off suit, but the man was elegant in a short black tux that fit him to perfection.

Popbottle adjusted a pair of reading glasses on his nose. "She was a friend to all of you, too, the kind of gracious lady who would mend your shirt, babysit your child, or bring chicken soup if you fell ill. And in the doing, she would pat your hand and say a prayer, listen to your troubles, and always, always leave you with a smile and a sense of hope.

"When Lydia loved, she loved forever. She loved this town, her home, her garden. She loved her family, especially Sloan, who was more son than nephew. Her pride in this strapping young man was immense, and she was never happier than when she was with him. England, Hawaii, Japan—she enjoyed their many trips, but most of all she enjoyed being with her nephew. He brought color to her cheeks and a bounce to her step. An old man like me could get downright jealous."

A quiet chuckle rippled through the mourners and the lump in Sloan's throat grew larger.

"For those of us fortunate enough to call her friend for a lifetime, she was a light. Some friends glow bright and then flicker out with time. Lydia's light was a steady glow filled with warmth and goodwill that I will carry with me the rest of my life."

He paused, unfolded a white handkerchief from his pocket and dabbed at the corners of his eyes. Sloan clasped his hands tightly together and leaned forward. His heart pounded like war drums, threatening to break out of his chest and splash tears on his face. He'd faced some difficult moments in his life, but this one ranked near the top of the list.

After a few seconds, Ulysses Jones regained his composure, cleared his throat and continued. "Most of all, Lydia loved her God, a steadfast faith that carried her through the sorrows of life with grace, elegance and beauty. And it is in her love of God today that we find comfort. Lydia believed with all her heart that to be absent from the body is to be present with her Lord. So to Sloan, as well as to dear Annie, who cared for Lydia faithfully during the last year of her life, my message is simple. Love as she loved. Give as she gave, remembering that the legacy of our dear Lydia will live on through you."

Professor Ulysses "Popbottle" Jones stepped down from the podium and shook hands with Sloan before making his way to the casket. He placed a beribboned spray of lilies of the valley amidst the pink roses, and then with glassy eyes and great dignity, exited the building.

Sloan sat on the veranda, legs stretched out on the plank porch, tie loosened, suit jacket off, although he'd not bothered to change clothes. Upstairs his employees were making themselves comfortable and he was grateful to Annie for helping prepare the seldom-used guest rooms. Tara had opted for a room at Redemption Motel, compliments of Kitty Wainright.

He was grateful to Annie for a lot of things, the least of which was her stalwart support during today's funeral. Now she was present at his request, though he'd told himself to let her go. Using Lydia's death as a ploy for keeping Annie close was a shameless thing to do. If he was half a man, he'd get on a plane tomorrow with Tara, Mack and Harrison and leave Annie alone. He should get back to work and the real world anyway. The idea didn't excite him as much as he'd expected it to.

But there was Justin. He still hadn't resolved that issue. Probably never would completely. No matter how many years had passed, the fact remained. Sloan had abandoned his unborn child and the girl he'd claimed to love. Even if God forgave a sin of that magnitude, He shouldn't.

Annie's job as Lydia's caregiver was over. She no longer *had* to be here, but she remained.

He wondered if that meant anything other than her dedication to his aunt and her innate kindness to anyone in need.

"You don't have to stay," he blurted when she came through the French doors.

She hesitated, one hand on the wicker rocker across from him. "Are you asking me to leave?"

"No." He never wanted her out of his sight. "I'm giving you an option. You don't work here anymore. There's nothing to hold you."

She gave him a strange look. "I could say the same for you."

The truth of the statement cut into his soul. He was no one now. There were no Hawkinses left except for him and a boy who carried Hawkins blood but someone else's name. Sloan's roots were buried with Lydia. "I'm going to finish the garden before I sell the house."

Suddenly pensive, Annie went to the railing and gazed out over the half-completed garden. "Lydia would be overjoyed to hear you say that. She longed for weddings in the garden again."

Annie was still attired in the jade dress that brushed the tops of her calves and shaped her figure. Her blond hair had pulled loose from a clip and the ever-present breeze flirted with the stray locks. He wanted to touch her hair. Touch her. Hold her and take care of her.

But he was about twelve years too late for that. She was wary of him. He was wary, too, mostly of himself. After the events of the day, he felt directionless.

"Restoring the garden seems right. Even when I sell the house, the garden will live on."

Annie turned from the railing. "You're really going to sell, then?"

"What else can I do with an old house in Oklahoma?"

Annie wrapped her fingers around the top of the white railing. The flirtatious wind tossed a few strands of hair across her mouth. Sloan resisted the urge to go to her and pull them away. Looking at her mouth brought back the kiss.

He hoped his feelings didn't show on his face. He glanced to the side.

"What about Justin?" she asked quietly.

His gaze snapped back to hers. Green eyes bored into him. He wanted her to ask "What about us," but she hadn't. She'd asked about their son. The boy's needs were far more important than his. Trouble was Sloan had no clue what Justin needed.

"I don't want him hurt by this town. They won't be nice if they discover he was sired by that Hawkins boy."

"You might be surprised."

He doubted it. "He's helping restore the garden. He can take pride in that. Even if no one else knows the truth, Justin will know this is his heritage. The Hawkins name used to matter—Lydia and her parents and grandparents helped build this town. That's all I can give him."

Annie gave him a long, searching look. "Maybe it is."

And he wondered what she meant.

She stepped away from the rail and settled in the rocker. A hummingbird hovered like a tiny helicopter over the vacated space before zooming toward the rose arbor.

"I remember your mother, Sloan. She was a good person, too. Don't forget that part of who you are. When I was small, Daddy would take me into the diner for pie. Joni knew my favorite was banana cream and always served it with a free piece of bubblegum on the side. I'm sure she paid for that herself. And she'd talk to me as if I was somebody important, not just a little girl tagging along with her daddy. She was a lot like Lydia in that respect."

Sloan had never made the comparison. "I guess she was.

She's been gone so long sometimes I forget the details of the time we had together. But I know she loved me." He chuckled softly and held his arms out to the side. "Hey, what's not to love?"

Annie didn't go there. "Don't you wonder where she went and what became of her?"

"Sure. I wonder where she's living—*if* she's still living— if she married and had other kids. If she's happy. Mostly, I wonder why. I could never accept that she would abandon me the way she did."

"But there's no other explanation. Her clothes were gone and so was she."

"Yes." He sighed. "She could have left a note." The memory of that last night surfaced, familiar because he'd relived it hundreds of times. "She promised to take me fishing. Up until that night, Mama had always kept her promises."

Annie stopped rocking. "I agree. That part is odd."

"I think so, too."

"Maybe she forgot. Or maybe she was caught up in the moment."

"Maybe," he said, a tad morosely. "If she forgot, it was the only time."

"Tell me again what you remember. I've heard a mix of stories over the years until I can't sort fact from fiction."

"That's Redemption," Sloan said, surprised not to feel bitter. God must really be working on him. Or maybe he was too mentally exhausted from the funeral to muster up the resentment. "The night she left, there was a man in the living room with her. She knew I worried when she let people come to the house late at night and crash on the couch. I know what other people thought, but Mama wasn't…what they said. She had a big heart. Her family had died in a car accident and she said she'd never forgive herself if she let a drunk drive and somebody else was killed the way her parents were. So she'd take a guy's keys and let him sleep it off on the couch."

"The man you saw was drunk?"

"That's the weird thing. He wasn't. And he wasn't the usual type Mama brought home."

"What do you mean?"

"He was fancier." He shrugged. "I told your dad all this the next day but he didn't find anyone fitting my description. I was a kid. My observations were too vague." The diner had called Chief Dooley when the dependable Joni didn't report for work. The chief had picked Sloan up from school and told him his mother had apparently left town during the night. Sloan, accustomed to getting himself off to school, had assumed his mother had gone in at six for her usual shift. "The man wore a blue dress shirt and dark slacks. Most of Mama's visitors were regular guys, truckers, laborers. They didn't dress up. This guy wore a fancy turquoise bracelet. I remember distinctly thinking it was a sissy piece of jewelry for a man, and that Mama was safe with a sissy."

"Maybe he was rich and promised her a better life."

"And he didn't want an eleven-year-old kid tagging along." With her husband in prison, Joni was a lonely woman struggling to make ends meet in a small, judgmental town. Life could not have been easy for her. Still, the idea that his mother could forget him stung. Perhaps that was why he'd never quite believed it.

"Oh, Sloan, I'm sorry, but that's the way it looked then and the way it looks now."

"I know." He rubbed the heels of his hands against his tired eye sockets. He'd not slept much in the past few days. "But I'm still puzzled by something else that didn't fit. Everyone said she left with a trucker she met at the diner."

"But no one remembered his name."

"Right. No one could pinpoint a specific trucker who'd been in the diner that night. And no one had seen Mama leave with anyone. She was a good mother. Why did she go without a word to anyone, especially her only child?"

"Back then, I never thought about it, but now her actions seem out of character to me, too."

"I've tried to figure it out for years and come up empty every time. I suppose the puzzle will never be resolved. And Redemption will never forget."

They sat in thoughtful silence for a while, the heat fading with the day.

At one point, Tara came to the porch to announce the trio was going for pizza. Annie had laughed. The house was filled with food and the Virginians wanted pizza. After his friends departed, Sloan and Annie talked about the funeral, about Lydia, about life in general.

With Annie sitting next to him, rocking slowly back and forth in Lydia's chair, Sloan's imagination went crazy. There were so many unanswered questions between them—questions that, like his mother's disappearance, would never be answered—but he couldn't help wishing he could freeze the moment. Being with Annie felt right. It always had.

He wanted so much to tell her everything.

Love warred with truth. Would telling her the truth about that long ago night hurt her more? Or make things right between them?

"Annie." His shirtsleeve whispered against wicker as he reached across the short space and twined his fingers with hers.

She turned toward him, green eyes serene and curious. In the garden, bees buzzed and a gentle, hopeful breeze coaxed fragrance from the blossoms.

Annie's cell phone rang, vibrating against the metal patio table. She withdrew her hand from his to answer. "Hello?

Dad?" She slanted a glance toward Sloan. "Yes, I am. Don't worry about it, okay?"

Her shoulders drooped in annoyance and she rolled her eyes but got up from the chair and turned her back to Sloan. Her voice was low and intense. "Today was the funeral, Daddy. Don't you have any compassion?"

Compassion. Right. Sloan didn't have to be a genius to decipher the content of their conversation. He got the message. Chief Dooley didn't want his daughter hanging out at the Hawkins' house even on the day of a funeral.

The call ended and Annie snapped the phone shut with a little too much force. She came back to the wicker rocker but didn't sit. The call had clearly agitated her. "What were you about to say?"

Jaw tight, Sloan shook his head. Some things were better kept inside. "Nothing important."

Chapter Ten

"Who was that gorgeous redhead?"

Annie and her friend, Jilly Fairmont, a redhead herself, browsed the racks at Zinnia's, the only clothing store in Redemption. They'd been rehashing the week's events, including Lydia's funeral and the restoration of the Wedding Garden. Justin was working with Sloan as usual, and Delaney skipped around Zinnia's, talking to everyone in the place.

"Her name is Tara. She works for Sloan's security company."

"Works for him?" Jilly looked doubtful. "Are you jealous?"

Annie pretended interest in an orange tank top. "Of course not. Why would I be?"

Then why had her stomach clenched the moment she'd seen the petite Tara clinging to Sloan's elbow?

"Oh, please, Annie, spare me the pretense. This is your BFF you're talking to. I know all your secrets."

Well, not all of them. "Sloan and I are old news. I wish everyone would understand that and stop trying to push us together."

"Then why are you still hanging around the Hawkins'

place? And why do your cheeks flush and your eyes light up whenever I mention his name?"

She was asking herself the same questions. The answer was simple. Annie Markham was an idiot. "Lydia worried about how Sloan would handle her death. She asked me to be there for him. I'm a friend helping a friend through a difficult time. As a nurse, that's my job."

"As simple as that?"

"Yes." There was nothing simple about her confused mass of feelings about and for Sloan Hawkins. Using Lydia's request was her best excuse. She *had* promised, though being with Sloan every day was harder and better than she'd imagined. His learning about Justin further complicated the issue. She definitely felt something for him. With all her heart, she prayed it was only friendship.

"Very nice of you to be so compassionate. I'm sure Sloan appreciates having his old flame at his beck and call." Annie whacked her with a hanger, and Jilly's freckled nose wrinkled in laughter. "I think it's kind of romantic. Mr. Tall, Dark and Dangerously Handsome comes back to town after all these years to find his first love divorced and lonely, just waiting for him to sweep her off her feet."

"You watch too many Hallmark movies." Annie yanked a skirt from the rack and held the beige cotton against her body. "I am not lonely. I have two active kids, a busy church, a demanding career, plenty of friends."

"And no boyfriend. Not one date since Joey the Jerk hit the trail." Jilly yanked the skirt from her hands and jammed it back on the rack. "Too frumpy."

"I'm *not* lonely," Annie insisted, riffling through the skirts some more. "I don't have time for dates. My life is full."

"Why don't you ask Sloan out? I dare you."

"Jilly! I'm going home if you don't stop. Besides, my father would have a fit."

"Oh, for goodness' sake, Annie. You're a grown woman."

"Tell my dad that."

Jilly laughed. "I'll pass."

"That's what I figured." Annie took a white blouse from the rack. "What do you think of this one?"

"Too frumpy."

"Would you stop saying that? I'm a nurse and a Christian. I dress modestly."

"Dressing modestly is not the same as living in scrubs and wearing your grandma's cast-offs." Jilly extracted a satiny turquoise button-up. "Try this. It'll look great with your eyes and show off that curvy figure."

"Ooh, that is pretty."

With her usual exuberance, Jilly wiggled her eyebrows and said, "I'm sure Sloan would agree."

Annie rolled her eyes. "He's going back to Virginia soon."

"After the house sells and the garden is completed," Jilly shot back. "Which could take months."

"Jilly, seriously. I don't need the grief. Sloan will leave. That's the whole point. I can't take another loss. Let it go, okay?"

Jilly's bow mouth dropped open. "Oh, wow."

"What's that supposed to mean?"

"I was just kidding around, but—" Jilly cocked her head to one side, a hand to her hip "—oh, Annie. Girl, girl, girl. You're in love with Sloan Hawkins."

The next afternoon Annie cleaned and sorted the medical equipment inside Lydia's old bedroom. The medical supply company was coming to pick up the oxygen bottles and other reusable objects in a while.

From here she could see outside. She thought about how

much Lydia had enjoyed watching the progress in the garden and ached with missing her patient and friend. The old Victorian seemed quiet and sad without her.

She went to the window. Delaney had ingratiated herself with Sloan to the point that he'd hired her, too. Annie figured the child was in the way, but Sloan claimed she added an element of cheer and was a terrific gofer. Delaney had giggled, thinking he meant a small, furry rodent. At the moment, the nine-year-old dangled by her knees from a maple branch, singing at the top of her lungs, her long, pale ponytail pointing toward the ground.

Meanwhile, Justin did the real work. He lugged a large pot of something toward the far end of the garden. She was proud of her son. After he'd paid restitution for the broken windows, he kept working for Sloan by choice.

She sighed. *Sloan.* Every other thought was of him.

Jilly was right. She'd fallen in love with him despite her best intentions not to. But he hated this town and he would leave again. He'd told her as much.

Early this morning his guests had returned to Virginia, but not before Annie had noticed an undercurrent between Sloan and the beautiful Tara.

Well, who was she kidding? Sloan was an attractive man. Naturally, he'd have girlfriends.

She wondered why he'd never married.

He came into sight around a flowering shrub. T-shirt plastered to his body, face glistening with sweat and smudges of dirt, he tossed an arm over Justin's shoulders. Annie's heart fluttered like the butterfly feasting on the magenta blooms.

Father and son.

Part of her was glad for the attention Sloan had given their child. Justin had desperately needed a strong male in his life. Another part worried about what would happen once Sloan returned to Virginia. She'd tried to broach the subject with both of them and gotten nowhere.

Joey had already wounded Justin, and Annie's father hadn't helped with his tough cop mentality. Would another rejection shatter her child completely?

She'd have to try talking to Sloan again.

The hair on the back of Sloan's neck tingled. He dropped his arm from Justin's shoulders and glanced at the veranda. She wasn't there.

He scanned the side of the house, coming to a stop at Lydia's window. The quick stab of sorrow snagged his breath. Lydia wasn't there, either.

"She wouldn't want you to be sad."

Sloan pivoted toward his son. Like him, Justin was a sweaty, dirty mess. "When did you become a mind reader?"

"Miss Lydia told me." His shoulder hitched. "Sometimes she'd make me read to her and she'd tell me stuff."

"Make you?"

"You know. She liked to hear me. Said I reminded her of you."

The idea of his aunt patiently nurturing his son squeezed Sloan's heart. "She knew about you even before I did."

"Yeah?"

"Yeah." Sloan stood in silence taking in the house the Hawkins family had called home for over a century. There were a lot of secrets in that old house, a lot of love and laughter and living, too. If only walls could talk.

"Mom was standing at the window a minute ago."

Sloan removed a glove and whacked the dirt against his thigh. Was he that obvious? "She's been a good friend helping me out."

Balancing on his toes, Justin crouched next to a perennial bed and pinched the dead head of a coneflower. "You could take her out for pizza or steak or something. Pay her back."

"Better not."

Justin tossed the wilted flower aside and stood, dusting his already filthy hands on his jeans shorts. "Why?"

He knew the question went deeper than a steak dinner. "I can't stay in Redemption, Justin."

"Why not?"

"Life is complicated. I'll explain it to you someday." *When I figure it out for myself.*

"Don't you like my mom?"

Sloan sighed. The kid was killing him. "Your mom's great. I'll expect you to take care of her and Delaney after I leave."

The belligerent expression, gone most of the time of late, returned. "I'm just a dumb kid."

"A kid, yes. Dumb, no way. Chip off the old block, remember?" He clapped a hand on Justin's back. "You gonna be okay when I return to Virginia?"

The boy looked down, kicked a dirt clod. "Will you come back?"

Now there was a sticky question. "Maybe."

"So if you're leaving anyway, what could it hurt to take my mom out for pizza? I mean, as a thank-you gift, sort of?"

Sloan laughed. "See? I told you you're not dumb. Come on, let's finish planting those butterfly bushes before you get us both in hot water."

The old-fashioned Redemption Hardware and Tack Store smelled exactly as Sloan remembered. He stopped in the doorway as nostalgia overwhelmed him. Axle grease, burned coffee and power tools—a man's paradise. As a boy, he'd hung around the back waiting for a chance to help load a stove or other heavy item for a few cents' tip. On especially hot days the owner, Simmy-John Case, descendent of the town's founder, bought him a bottle of pop.

A head poked around the jumbled end cap of one aisle. Except for a few lines and a few extra pounds, Simmy-John hadn't changed much. His hair was still black as ink and he still limped from a war wound. "Be with you in a minute, Sloan."

A man didn't get that kind of personal attention in the new megastores. Until now, he'd resented the notoriety but lately—well, lately the town seemed different. Death made people kind.

Expecting to find the lawnmower blades on his own, he waved the man away, though Simmy-John's lined face had already disappeared. "No hurry."

As though his subconscious remembered the store's layout, Sloan headed toward the west side of the building past a bin overflowing with a hodgepodge of red bike reflectors, mismatched drawer knobs, and silver mailbox stencils. Green bread-loaf shaped mailboxes lined up next to oscillating fans and electric screwdrivers. He found the mower blades and carried them to the check-out counter near the back of the store, where three men leaned on their elbows, talking to the proprietor. One was an older farmer in jean overalls—Orville Warp. Another was Jace Carter, the quiet local contractor. The last was G.I. Jack, though Popbottle Jones was nowhere in sight.

"How you been, Sloan?" Simmy-John asked, making no move to check him out. Being "neighborly" was part of small-town etiquette. Rushing in and out without a real good excuse was considered rude.

"Doing pretty good. Yourselves?" Sloan's greeting took in the group. Except for Jace, they were men he remembered from childhood.

"Fine as frog hair," Simmy-John answered. "Sure was sorry about your Aunt Lydia. A finer woman never drew breath."

"Funeral service was nice," G.I. interjected. He was sorting through a pile of bolts and screws.

"How is Mr. Jones?" Sloan asked.

If G.I. was surprised at the question, he didn't show it. "He's all right. A little down."

Sloan understood too well. "Tell him I asked about him."

"Drop in anytime and tell him yourself."

"I just might do that."

Orville threaded thick fingers through his suspenders. "Heard you were opening the Weddin' Garden again."

A little taken aback at the rumor, Sloan fiddled with the shrink-wrap packaging. "No, just doing some upkeep."

"Is that a fact? Well, that's not what we heard," Simmy-John said, taking the mower blades from Sloan. "I was just going to ask if you're booking weddings yet. My daughter—I don't know if you remember Sunny—she has her heart set on having a wedding in the garden just like me and her mama."

Sloan remembered Sunny Case, but he couldn't imagine the popular former cheerleader remaining single this long. She was close to his age.

"We still have a lot of work left to do, though I'm trying. Lydia wanted the garden restored and I'm determined to see it through before the place sells."

"Pretty big task by yourself."

"You're right. It is. I've thought about hiring more, but I have a good helper." Though, the garden was slow in coming and the work needed to be finished soon or left undone, the fact remained Sloan liked spending one-on-one time with Justin this way. He'd learned a lot about the boy, the town and even Annie. Having Justin around kept Annie close, as well.

How pathetic an admission was that?

Simmy-John pointed a scanning device at the back of the mower blades and a beep sounded. "Heard that, too. Annie

Markham's boy. He's a pistol, ain't he? Always into one thing or the other. Needs his britches fanned, I'm thinking, but Chief Dooley covers up for him since his daddy run off."

Sloan took offense at the remark. "Justin's a little rough around the edges, but he's a good kid. And he works hard. If I had ten more like him, the garden would be open by fall."

Orville sipped coffee from a disposable cup before tossing it in a trash can. "Did you say you were selling the Hawkins estate?"

"That's the plan." He figured on having a sale to liquidate the furniture, but first he had to go through everything, remove personal items, photos, papers, and make decisions on what to keep. The thought of the task ahead depressed him enough that he'd been putting it off to work on the garden instead.

"A Hawkins has owned that land since the Run," Simmy-John said. "Won't seem right with new owners. Sure you won't change your mind and stay on?"

The question bewildered Sloan. He never expected anyone in Redemption to actually want him to live in the house again. "My business is in Virginia."

"Exactly what kind of business are you in, Sloan? We've heard different things."

Sloan laughed and told them, mulling the fact that he wasn't offended by the nosiness. According to the gossip from Annie, he was evil on a motorcycle, selling drugs to babies or gambling away his inheritance like his daddy.

G.I. scooped a handful of black screws and dumped them into a paper cup. "I coulda told you that, Orville. Sloan is a security expert. If you want someone to guard your backside, he's the man. Heard he was mighty good at it, too. Saved a senator from an assassin a while back."

The detail had been protecting a Supreme Court justice, but

Sloan didn't bother to correct G.I.'s story. He'd never wanted to care what any of them thought about his lifestyle, but a glow of pleasure warmed his belly at the complimentary responses.

Simmy-John, however, was stuck on getting his daughter married in Lydia's backyard. "What if you sell the house and the new owners won't let folks have weddings there?"

Sloan hadn't thought that far ahead. The fact that no weddings had taken place in the garden for several years seemed a moot point. "A lawyer might be able to write up a contract to that effect."

Simmy-John handed over the mower blades in exchange for Sloan's credit card. "That'll be twenty-eight dollars and ninety-two cents. Still don't seem right selling out."

Selling didn't seem right to Sloan either, but what else could he do?

By the time he returned to the house, Annie had finished her work and gone, along with the two children. Sloan roamed through the big, rambling house, completely alone for the first time since Lydia's death. Everywhere he looked memories lurked, waiting to jump out and grab him. The sooner he could sell, the sooner he could banish these feelings.

If not for the personal nature of having someone else riffle through Lydia's things, he'd hire a service to come in and do the job. Annie had offered to help with the task of boxing and sorting. Funny, but she was the only person other than himself he trusted to do the work. She was on vacation, she claimed, taking some time off between assignments. Losing Lydia had hit her hard, too.

She should go somewhere, take a rest, enjoy herself. He thought of the trips he and Lydia had enjoyed together, a lump welling in his chest. Had Annie ever taken a vacation? Had Joey taken her and the kids to Yellowstone or Disney World?

From what he'd learned about their marriage, probably not. He wondered what she'd say if he offered to take her little family on a trip.

He wandered down the hall toward the back of the house and the library where he'd once done his homework in front of the fireplace.

If he offered to pay for a vacation, sort of as a bonus for taking such good care of Lydia, would Annie be insulted?

"Lord," he murmured, knowing there wasn't another soul to hear. "What am I going to do about all this? The house. Annie. Justin. Life was a lot simpler before I came home."

Simpler, yes, but emptier, too, if he'd admit the truth. Here in this town he'd despised, he'd begun a budding relationship with God as well as with his son. He would never regret either.

The wall phone in the kitchen jangled, half a house away. Lydia had never put in an extension. He let it ring into silence, not in the mood to talk to anyone, especially a telemarketer.

In the library, he found the stack of boxes he'd collected. No time like the present to begin sorting through his family, although he'd leave his bedroom and the kitchen until last. He didn't know when he'd be able to face Lydia's upstairs rooms, the ones where she'd basically lived until her illness forced her downstairs. He'd spent many hours in that suite of rooms, watching her quilt in the sunny sewing nook, listening to her advice or whining on her shoulder.

The house was large, with an attic and basement as well as two floors of high-ceilinged rooms and cubby holes, all filled with more than a century of stuff. Packing would take a while.

He began where he was, taking dusty books from the shelves. Some were familiar, others not. He paused to leaf through one and found an inscription from his grandfather to his grandmother scribbled in the flyleaf. Gently, he put the volume in a box he'd marked to keep.

He reached for the photo albums, curious about the Hawkinses who'd come before him. The first volume stunned him.

"Clayton Hawkins." Sloan ran a hand over the embossed name and a photo of a handsome young man with dark hair and blue eyes. "Dad." The name sounded strange on his lips. "I never even knew you."

He opened the cover and a pile of letters tumbled out, all marked with the return address of the Oklahoma State Penitentiary. His father had gone to prison for murder when Sloan was two and had died there a few years later. If his mother had kept in contact with her husband, Sloan never knew about it. But Lydia apparently had never forgotten the brother she'd babied and spoiled.

Mesmerized, Sloan put the letters aside for later reading and began to page through the scrapbook he hadn't known existed. Photos of childhood birthday parties and circus trips gave way to faded yellow newspaper clippings that chronicled band concerts, football games and a class presidency. Clayton Hawkins had not always been bad.

Why hadn't anyone told his son? Had the relationship between Sloan's mother and Lydia been too contentious to allow a boy access to his father's memory?

Vaguely, he heard a noise in the front of the house, but remained focused on stories of the Clayton Hawkins he hadn't known. Noise in the old house was a common event.

He sneezed and a voice said, "Bless you."

With a start, he looked up to find Annie standing in the arched doorway. As usual, his belly did that clenching thing.

"Are you okay?" She asked that a lot lately.

He dropped his propped feet to the floor. "When did you take up breaking and entering?"

"You didn't answer the phone."

"That was you? Were you worried?" He kind of liked the idea.

She cocked her head to one side. A lock of hair bunched on her shoulder. "No, Sloan, I drove across town late at night to borrow a cup of sugar. Of course I was concerned. You've had a devastating loss."

He grinned and wiped a dusty hand down the front of his T-shirt. "I like it when you talk sassy."

"You bring out the worst in me."

The comment slapped him. He lost his sense of humor. "I'm sorry."

"Don't be. Jilly says I'm getting boring."

"You?" Sloan frowned. If she got any less boring, he would lose his mind. "Not happening."

"What are you doing back here?"

"Packing."

Her face closed up. "Oh."

"I have to do this, Annie."

Her silence frustrated him. What did she expect? That he'd keep a house he couldn't live in and torture himself with thoughts of coming home again? "Where are Delaney and Justin?"

"In the yard chasing fireflies."

A flood of memories came with her statement. He could almost see Lydia standing on the veranda with a fruit jar in hand while a laughing boy raced around the yard capturing the hapless insects. Only this time, the boy in his mind wasn't him. It was Clayton Hawkins.

"Let's go help them."

"You're kidding."

But Sloan was already getting up from the sofa. "Come on, pretty girl. Come out and play."

He stretched out a palm, waiting, hoping.

Annie hesitated only a moment. Then a slow smile elevated her killer cheekbones. "Promise not to jump out and scare me?"

He waggled his eyebrows. "What do you think?"

She laughed and placed her hand in his.

Chapter Eleven

They'd stayed up too late. Annie had enjoyed every minute of chasing fireflies and her children and Sloan around the yard. She hadn't laughed that much in years. And Sloan was the boy she remembered minus the anger simmering beneath the surface. For that little while, he'd made her feel young and carefree and silly again.

She knew she was setting herself up for a hard fall, but Jilly was right. She'd been focused on working and caring for her kids and patients for so long, she'd become boring. She'd forgotten how good it felt to laugh and have fun with the people she cared about.

She glanced across the library where Sloan was sitting cross-legged on the hardwood floor going through papers. He hadn't shaved this morning, and in the disreputably ragged jeans that Justin considered too cool for words and a surprisingly tidy white T-shirt, Sloan did things to her heart that she'd forgotten existed. Good things. Things a woman needed to feel.

Last night, she'd prayed all the way home. She didn't want to be hurt again but the old adage that "it is better to have loved and lost than never to have loved at all" rang in her head. She'd been down that road before. Though the aftermath had been devastating and she would certainly do some things differently, if given the choice, wouldn't she still have loved the wild teenage Sloan?

She sighed and the sound must have been loud because Sloan glanced up and grinned. "Tired already?"

"No." She rotated a neck crick. "A little."

"Did I keep you up too late?"

"You know you did." She dusted off an ancient volume of Wordsworth before opening the cover.

"I had fun."

"Me, too."

He tossed a yellowed envelope into the trash can at his side. "We could do it again. Maybe. If you want to."

"I don't know if I'm up to playing tag in the dark again."

He laughed. "How about a movie? You, me, the kids. There's a family film playing at the Twin Theater. Wanna go?"

Was he asking for a date?

When she only stared at him, his voice cajoled. "Let me take you out for dinner and a movie. If not here in Redemption, then wherever you say. I owe you that much."

He could have left out the last line. Actually, he could have left out the entire last comment. She didn't want him to feel obligated. Nor did she want him to feel embarrassed to be seen with her.

"You don't have to repay a kindness, Sloan. I'm helping because I want to. Lydia was my friend."

His hands stilled on the stack of papers. "Is that what you think? That I'm asking out of obligation?"

"Aren't you?" Annie caught her lower lip between her teeth, dismayed at the hurt in her answer.

Sloan shoved the cardboard box aside. It made a scraping sound against the hardwood. He got up and stalked toward her, eyes glittering like sapphire. Her pulse jitterbugged.

"Listen to me, pretty girl. I don't do things out of obligation. I do them because I want to. What I want more than anything is to take you somewhere nice, to see you dressed up in that jade dress again with your hair curving around your cheekbones and your face full of laughter." He touched her cheek. Annie shivered. Sloan's voice dropped to a whisper. "I want you to be happy."

Annie swallowed, mouth gone dry. What in the world did he mean? And didn't he know that a portion of her happiness dwelled with him and always had?

She moistened paper-dry lips. Sloan noticed and bracketed her face with his hard fingers, holding her frozen with that single, tender action. He stared into her eyes until her bones melted and she yearned to kiss him, not in comfort but in love.

She wondered what he was thinking and why he was saying such sweet things. Was it possible he felt something for her, too? Something more than obligation and gratitude. Something that had nothing to do with sharing a son.

Resisting the urge to circle her arms around his trim waist, she hooked her hands over his biceps. The grandfather clock ticked. As if that was his signal, Sloan pulled her up on tiptoes and touched his lips to hers. When the kiss ended, far too soon for Annie, he drew her against his chest and sighed. Being held by Sloan was like coming home.

"Whoever said you were boring hasn't kissed you," he murmured.

Annie laughed softly. "You like my jade dress?"

"Mmm-hmm. I like you in it. Gives you cat eyes."

"I'm not sure that's a compliment."

"That's because you're not a man. Thank the good Lord." A chuckle rumbled from his chest to her ear and she giggled again.

"We aren't getting any work done." Not that she was struggling to get away.

She felt his breath on her hair and the undeniable touch of lips against her scalp. "Break time. Better check on Justin and Delaney before they come looking for us."

"Oh, my, you're right." Stepping away, she pressed a hand to her warm cheek, horrified that for a few brief moments, she'd forgotten about her own children. Either could have walked in and found her kissing Sloan. She didn't have answers for the questions such discovery would bring. She wasn't sure herself what was going on. How could she explain to her children?

"I'll go," she said, eager to get her bearings and think about what had just transpired.

"Hey, wait a minute."

She pivoted at the doorway. "What?"

"You want steak or pizza?"

"Steak." A smile bloomed. "You can afford it."

His eyes crinkled. "Nothing like a sassy-mouthed woman."

Annie stuck out her tongue. As she headed down the hallway, she heard him call, "You kiss good, too."

Feeling light, she took juice boxes out to the kids, where Delaney was actually helping her brother plant a small bed of multicolored flowers along the edge of the porch. "How's it going out here?"

"We'll never get finished," Justin groused. "The more we do, the more we find that needs doing. Sloan should have hired a real gardener."

"Why not take a break until he comes out to help?"

"Nah, Delaney and I wanted to surprise him by having this bed finished."

Sloan's voice came from the porch. "I'm surprised. Good job."

Delaney, seeing her opportunity to escape work, dropped the trowel and skipped over to sling her arms around Sloan's knees. He patted her back, though his gaze remained on Justin and Annie.

"Give me a second to grab my gloves and I'll join you. Annie, do you mind working on the library without me?" A teasing grin played around his mouth and she knew he was thinking about the kiss.

For orneriness, she fluttered a hand over her heart. "I may pine away forever without you."

The grin widened. He tugged her hair as she flounced past him on the steps. She whirled around to say something silly, saw Justin watching them with bright interest and changed her mind. She was confused enough without dragging her son into the fray.

"Mommy, who is *that?*" Delaney had gone to the picket fence and was looking between the slats. "A bunch of cars are outside. I think it's Pastor Parker. And Zoey! Mom, Zoey is here."

Delaney bolted through the gate and disappeared. Annie changed direction and retreated down the steps and out to the fence to determine the identity of their unexpected visitors.

"Sloan," she said, unable to believe what she was seeing. "I think you had better come look at this."

Sloan's adrenaline jacked. Annie's voice sounded weird. In a career of watching other people's backs, he'd learned to trust his instincts. Something unusual was going on out in the street.

"What's up?" He casually jogged to the gate, where he could already see someone approaching.

Annie unhooked the gate latch and a trail of people entered the garden area, led by Kitty Wainright and Jace Carter. Out on the street more car doors slammed and voices rose, coming nearer. Delaney and her best friend, the vet's daughter Zoey, skipped across the yard holding hands. He would forever be amazed at the blind child's grace and ease in a sighted world.

"What is all this?" Annie asked.

Kitty, toting a rake, paused on the half-finished pathway. "We all got to talking about how wonderful it is that Sloan wants to restore the Wedding Garden in Lydia's memory. Then Simmy-John said you needed some help, so here we are. A garden party, if you will." Kitty laughed, a trill as pretty as birdsong. "Put us to work."

Well, blast him with a Taser. Redemption wanted to help *him?* "A garden party? As in landscaping work?"

Kitty's blond head bobbed with enthusiasm. "Yes, indeed. Just think how amazing it will be to have weddings here again, knowing we pitched in to make it happen. Now, what first?"

Sloan blinked at the accrued group of excited, eager faces and then at the unending landscape, too stunned to delegate. These people were here for him? To help him? He couldn't take it in. "I don't know."

"I do." The no-nonsense Mrs. Miller from the plant farm came striding up with a paper diagram in hand. "These are the plans you and I mapped out. The two of us can direct traffic and the rest can do the grunt work." With a jolly laugh, the outdoorsy woman pointed at the half-finished path leading from the gate through the various beds. "I love telling people what to do. Jace, you start on the path and mend the back fence. That's your expertise. Kitty and Cheyenne will help you."

The quiet contractor, who had enough work-honed muscle to finish the job alone, arched an eyebrow toward the two women. Both nodded eagerly. Sloan noticed the way Jace's gaze lingered on Kitty Wainright. Must be something going on there. Not that Sloan was one to pry, but he was a man trained to notice things.

"Trace will be here after work unless he has a call," Cheyenne said. She was a pretty woman, in a dark, intense kind of way, and a total opposite of Kitty Wainright's blond sweetness and light.

"He doesn't have to do that," Sloan protested. Cheyenne's new husband, Trace, was the county's only vet and as such worked long hours. "In fact, none of you have to do this. This is crazy."

"You don't want our help?" Simmy-John was already whacking at dead limbs. Pastor Parker was helping him.

"No. I mean, yes." He raked a hand through his hair. "If the garden is ever going to be finished, we can use some help, right, Justin?" He looked to the boy, whose face was as bewildered as his own.

"We're getting nowhere fast," Justin grumbled.

"Then get busy, son," the pastor said with a laugh. "You don't get volunteers like this every day."

Man, was that ever the truth. "I don't know what to say. I—"

But the crowd of about twenty volunteers was already fanning over the garden grounds like worker ants while Mrs. Miller shouted orders and the men called joking insults to one another. Apparently the supplies Sloan ordered had arrived, because Hank Martinelli from the Sugar Shack and Popbottle Jones carted in the wrought iron bench. Behind them, Ida June Click, the eighty-something handywoman in hot pink overalls and high-top tennis shoes, rolled a shiny red wheelbarrow. As she passed Sloan she poked a pink-gloved finger at him. "Many hands make light work."

"Yes, ma'am." The old woman's energy as well as her pithy sayings was legend.

Annie came up beside him and looped an arm through his elbow. "Close your mouth. You'll catch a bug."

He gazed down at her pretty face, remembering the kiss they'd shared only minutes ago. Today was an amazing day. "What are they doing?"

"Showing love in the only way they know how. Being neighborly."

Love. For him? For the Redemption bad seed? Nah, couldn't be. They'd come because of Lydia. And for her, he'd let them.

They went out for pizza.

Once the volunteers had loaded up for the day, the children set up a howl claiming starvation brought on by overwork. Too exhausted for anything fancy, they'd settled for the local pizza parlor.

It wasn't the romantic interlude Sloan had in mind. Annie didn't wear her green dress, but her eyes shone bright and happy and she laughed a lot. Contentment settled on him like a comfortable old sweatshirt.

"What a great day," Annie said as she took another slice of thick-crust pepperoni from the cardboard box. Delaney and Justin had already gobbled their pizza in favor of time at the video games. "Everyone working together like that—well, it's typical Redemption."

"Not to me." He was still stunned but feeling really warm and peaceful inside. Unbelievable. That's all he could think.

"As I've said before, your perception is skewed. Surely you can see that now."

"I'm starting to." Today had been a turning point of sorts, an answer to prayers he'd prayed in the dark of night for God to root out his bitterness. Interesting that the uprooting began in a garden full of well-meaning folks. "Did I mention how beautiful you look tonight?"

He reached across and brushed dusty parmesan from her cheek, mostly for an excuse to touch her. Today had been a turning point with Annie, too. A little voice in the back of his head kept hammering away with an impossible hope he didn't dare consider.

Annie laughed, and the blush over her cheekbones captivated him. He loved her more every day.

"Oh, yes," she said, "I'm stunning with my grass-stained capris and broken fingernails."

"Yeah, you are." And he meant it.

Delaney pranced up to her mother, white ponytail bobbing. Sloan thought she was the cutest little girl. "Can we have another quarter?"

Sloan reached in his pocket and handed her a bill. "Divide this with your brother, okay?"

"Thanks, Sloan. Wow! Justin will freak out." And she jitterbugged away toward the row of clanging, pinging video machines.

"You're spoiling them."

It felt good, too. When had he had anyone to dote on but a reluctant Aunt Lydia? "They worked hard."

"You'd spoil them anyway."

"Probably. They're great kids, Annie. You've done a good job."

"Even with Justin?" She sipped at her straw, eyes slanted toward him.

"Especially him. He's coming along." Justin was a deep kid who internalized his emotions. With Sloan he'd been opening up about his anger toward Joey and about a lot of guy stuff he wouldn't discuss with his mother. The trust had kept Sloan talking to God. Knowing what he knew about broken relationships, he didn't want to blow the chance to make a difference in his son's life.

"He idolizes you, Sloan." Pushing her Coke away, she picked at a piece of pepperoni. "I'm concerned."

"I know." The notion worried him, too. "I don't want to let him down."

Annie was silent but he knew her thoughts. She expected him to let them all down again. He didn't want to, but he probably would. The situation was impossible. Some days, days like today when Redemption embraced him with reminders of the good things about his childhood, he had aberrant thoughts of moving back, of throwing caution to the wind and asking Annie to try again. Police Chief Dooley Crawford was the fly in that delicious soup. To be with Annie, Sloan would have to tell her the truth about the reason he left Redemption in the first place. Learning about her father's conniving lies, lies that had forced her into a difficult marriage and left Justin without his biological father, would break her heart.

Leaving was just as bad.

With a sigh, he laced his fingers with hers and bounced their joined hands gently against the tabletop.

He and God had a lot more talking to do.

Chapter Twelve

"Look what I found." Sloan pushed back from an antique oak desk in the study where generations of Hawkinses had conducted business.

"Great minds think alike." Annie laughed and held up a handful of photos. She sat at a small table sorting old pictures into labeled boxes. "I have something to show you, too."

"All right, you first."

Sloan seemed different today. In fact, he'd seemed different last night at the pizza place. She credited some of the change to the volunteers, a few of whom planned to come again to finish the job. Sloan had been wonderfully touched, and she was glad. He deserved some redemption from the painful past.

After their pizza, when he'd taken her and the children home, Sloan had lingered at the door until Justin and Delaney headed to their rooms, and then he'd kissed her good-night.

Like a schoolgirl with a crush, her pulse fluttered at the memory. Twice yesterday he'd kissed her. Annie was old enough to know the times he brushed her hair from her eyes or touched her hand or her elbow or cheek were not accidents.

She couldn't help wondering what it meant. He cared for her, she was certain now, but there was hesitancy in him, too, as though he held something back. Regardless of her love and regardless of the son they shared, Annie was not fool enough to push a man into something he didn't want. So, she kept her love and her wishes to herself.

Today had been a day of discoveries as the two of them had sorted through boxes and closets and cupboards. Delaney and Justin had begged off and she'd taken pity on them, letting them stay at Mother's.

"Whatcha got?" he asked, coming to stand at her side. Before she could speak, he bent and touched his lips to hers.

"Sneaky," she said, breathless.

"Delicious," he said with a cheeky grin.

She fanned the selected photos across the table. All were old, but two were aged tintypes. "Look at these."

"They were taken in the garden."

"Probably among the first weddings to be held there, given how small the garden appears in comparison to today's landscape." She tapped a fingernail on one. "That's your great-great-aunt Hattie Jane Hawkins on her wedding day to Purvis Lee Blanchard."

One eyebrow hiked. "How do you know?"

"Says so on the back."

He braced both hands on the table and leaned in to peruse the row of pictures, bringing with him the scent of clean cotton and a morning shower. "The garden progresses in each one."

"That's what I was thinking, too. You can see how Hattie Jane's wedding has only a few bushes and flowers. Then with each photo, more and more is added over time until—" carefully watching his face, Annie flipped over the final photo "—this one, when the garden looks much as it does now."

Sloan was silent for a few seconds but a muscle beneath his eye ticked. "My parents."

Annie stroked his tense arm. "You've never seen this before, have you?"

He shook his head, throat working. "My parents were not discussed after Mama left. Whenever I tried to bring up the subject, Aunt Lydia would get teary-eyed. I never wanted to make her sad. So I stopped asking."

"They look happy, Sloan. That's important."

He studied the photo and his expression lightened. "They do, don't they? I never thought of them as happy together, but then I don't remember my dad at all."

"You know what I'm thinking?"

Smiling, he looked at her mouth and quirked an eyebrow. "Let me read your mind."

Feeling light and happy, as though they were standing on the precipice of something wonderful, she bopped his shoulder. "Behave."

"Do I have to?"

"Yes."

He sighed as if badly put-upon, but his blue eyes danced. "What?"

"Let's find all the photos of you and your parents that we can and make a scrapbook. You should know them better. Someday Justin will need that connection, too."

She thought he might refuse, but he didn't. "I'd like that. Now, let me show you what I found."

Sloan placed the ribbon-tied letters in front of Annie. He was having a lot of trouble with his emotions today. Yesterday the volunteers had nearly done him in with kindness and rattled his well-formed opinions of Redemption's citizens. Then last night, he'd kissed Annie again and never wanted to let her go. Now this morning as they cleaned out more of the rooms and his family roots began to show, he yearned to reconnect with the Hawkinses he'd never known. It was as though his very life's source resided within the walls of the old Victorian. Going home to the condo in Arlington held about as much appeal as living in Redemption once had.

Weird. This was just plain weird.

Annie had no idea what she'd started when she suggested gathering photos of his very lost childhood. None in the least. Suddenly, regaining memories of the childhood he'd tried to forget became very important. For his son and for himself.

"Are those letters?" Annie asked.

Sloan stared into green eyes as sweet as her kisses. Annie Markham was a force of nature strong enough to make him lose his good sense. "From Ulysses E. Jones to Aunt Lydia dating back nearly fifty years."

"No kidding. I always suspected they'd been in love, though neither ever said a word." She traced her fingers over the faded blue address. "This is quite a find."

"The question is why they never did anything but write letters. Not that I've read more than a couple." Invading someone's privacy—outside of business—wasn't his gig. "I think I should give these to Popbottle, don't you?"

"I think that would be a lovely gesture, Sloan." Annie's mouth curved, full, lush and tempting. He resisted the urge to kiss her again.

He pushed back, putting space between temptation and himself. He'd never been much good at resisting temptation. Ah, why bother to try. He wanted to be with her as long as he could. Maybe God would grant a miracle and he would never have to leave. The notion stunned him. What was he thinking? Of course he'd leave. He wanted to. He had to. Didn't he?

"Want to come with me?" he asked. "We could stop for dinner afterward."

Annie glanced at her watch. "Sorry. My mother is having a cookout with corn on the cob and homemade ice cream. I promised to be there by six."

Disappointment filtered through him. "Have fun."

"You could come, too." The statement was filled with hope.

He tried to joke. "You're having a cookout, not a shoot-out."

"Sloan."

Her heavy sigh settled in Sloan's chest like a bowling ball. He and the police chief would always have the past between them. Keeping it there was the only way to protect Annie—and that put Sloan right back where he'd started.

The house belonging to Popbottle Jones and his business partner G.I. Jack sat on a parcel of land not far from Redemption River. Sloan tucked the packet of letters into his saddle-bag and roared off in that direction. A couple of times he'd considered buying a car, mostly to mess with the police chief's mind, but so far he hadn't. Lydia's ancient Lincoln still ran when he hauled more than himself. Today, he needed a good, fast ride on his Harley, and hopefully Dooley was heading home for the cookout that Sloan could not attend.

Stupid how that hurt.

On the edge of town, he slowed near the diner where his mother had worked years ago. Since coming back, he'd avoided going inside. Maybe he would before he left again. Redemption Diner looked smaller than he remembered, and the parking lot between the narrow building and the bar next door was barely a strip of gravel. No wonder men stumbled from the bar to the diner for a chance to sober up on coffee and a late-night breakfast.

In a few minutes, he turned up the gravel road leading to Popbottle's place—a leaning frame house surrounded by the trappings one would expect from a pair of Dumpster divers. Two dogs charged out from beneath the board porch, yapping for all they were worth. Sloan braked the bike, coming to a halt beneath a scraggly shade tree. As he tossed a leg over the seat, a nanny goat skidded around the corner of the house, bleating.

Sloan's mood elevated. No one could come to this place without smiling.

"Arf!" he said to the dogs and laughed aloud when both yipped, fell to their bellies and crawled beneath the porch. The nanny goat, however, was not intimidated.

"I guess you're in charge," he said to her. She answered with a loud bleat as if in confirmation.

The front door, a blue painted mismatch to the house, scraped open. Popbottle Jones called out. "Sloan Hawkins, greetings and enter."

Taking the bundle, Sloan went inside. The interior was jam-packed with every conceivable piece of junk.

"How are you, Mr. Jones? I've been intending to come out and thank you again for Aunt Lydia's eulogy."

"My privilege, though a sad one to be sure. Would you care for a refreshment?"

"No, thanks. I have something I wanted to give you." Sloan extended the packet. "Actually, sir, they're yours to begin with. I'm simply returning them. And I apologize for reading a couple before realizing what they were."

The dignified old Dumpster diver tilted his head in curiosity but as he accepted the letters, recognition dawned. "I believe I shall sit down."

After taking the nearest chair, Popbottle stared at the pile of letters. Almost reverently, he opened one. The paper crinkled in his thick fingers as he read. Sloan remained silent, respectful as Popbottle slipped a finger beneath his glasses and rubbed.

"Where did you find these?" he asked at last, looking up at the still-standing Sloan.

"An old secretary in Lydia's study." And then unnecessarily, he added, "I'm cleaning out the house."

"To sell?"

"Yes."

Popbottle carefully laid the letters in his lap. "So you will leave us again?"

Sloan's defenses rose. "I don't live here. I'm just settling the estate for my aunt."

"So you say." Popbottle removed his glasses and rubbed the lenses on his shirttail. "What of Annie and the children?"

Sloan opened his mouth to give the standard denial, but heard himself say, "I love her."

"Of course you do. Anyone can look at the two of you together and know. She loves you, too."

Sloan sank into the only remaining unencumbered chair. "It won't work."

"May I inquire as to why?"

"Life. The past. Everything. It's too complicated."

Popbottle lifted the packet of letters. "I thought the same thing fifty years ago, Sloan, as did your aunt."

"What happened?" Elbows propped on his knees, Sloan steepled his fingers and leaned forward.

"As you say, life was complicated. I loved her. She loved me, and we discussed being wed in the Hawkins's garden." Popbottle Jones smiled a nostalgic smile. "I had wonderful visions of the future. So did she, but as we began to share, our dreams did not coincide. I, fool that I was, admired intellectual endeavors above all else. When the offer of an Ivy League professorship arrived, I asked her to go with me. She refused."

"Why?"

"Your father."

"My—"

Popbottle held up a silencing hand. "You must understand, my boy, Clayton was born very late in the life of your grand-parents. They had despaired of having any children other than Lydia, who was nearly grown when the baby arrived. Clayton, the long-awaited male heir, was spoiled and coddled by everyone, including his older sister."

"Aunt Lydia."

"Exactly. Sadly, the young master grew to be a spoiled and reckless youth. When your grandparents passed on, Lydia took charge of her brother."

"And wouldn't leave him behind."

"No, indeed. He needed her, she claimed, more than I, though she begged me to give up the professorship and remain in Redemption. Pride goeth before a fall, Sloan. Remember that. Wounded to the quick, I wrapped my cloak of pride around me and left Redemption behind, believing if Lydia loved me, she would choose me over Clayton."

"She didn't."

"No." He gently fingered the pages, his jowls sagging more than usual. Softly, he said, "She kept my letters. I never knew."

"And she never married."

"But I did—a girl more amenable to my pursuits than fair Lydia. A fine woman. We had a son and a daughter." He smiled softly. "After that, I was better able to understand Lydia's unyielding love for the brother she'd reared. In time, the marriage and academia soured, and I took to drink." The old gentleman rose from the chair and went to the doorway. "What happened next both destroyed and recreated me."

Sloan held his breath, aware that something terrible must

have happened to change a professor into a junk dealer. "You don't have to tell me."

"Ah, but I must." Popbottle turned back, eyes misty. "Drink is a terrible tyrant, Sloan, stronger than love for a woman or a child. One night, my little family and I attended a gathering. By evening's end I was badly inebriated but insisted on driving, though my wife tried to stop me."

Sloan's gut clenched. He knew what was coming.

"I missed a curve and killed them all." The dignified voice faded. "All but me."

"I'm sorry."

"Thank you. So am I, but regret did not change what had happened. I paid a fine and spent some time in jail, filled with a self-loathing that I cannot begin to describe. My life was over, my family and career gone. I took to the streets, wandering, lost and undone, and there I met Jesus. Eventually, Redemption called me home, and I knew, though I had greatly changed, my pride gone, my intellect wasted, I would be welcome here."

"Did Aunt Lydia know about all this?"

"No one in this town knows except G.I. Jack. But more than anyone, I could not bear for Lydia to know how low I had fallen. Drunkenness, negligent homicide. Neither are commendations."

"She must have known something had changed you."

"Certainly, but she had the grace never to broach the subject. As was her way, she accepted me as I am, although it took her illness to make me swallow my pride and approach her again."

"She had long ago forgiven you."

"Ah, yes. Forgiveness is a beautiful gift, but I struggled with accepting hers until it was too late."

"May I ask why you're telling me this?"

"Because, my dear boy, I loved the woman who loved you." He rose and gently placed a hand on Sloan's shoulder.

"For her sake and in her memory, I do not want you to make the same mistakes. When God presents a second chance, grasp hold for all you're worth and don't let go for anything."

Chapter Thirteen

The scent of grilled chicken basted in Italian seasonings drifted over the redbrick patio in Dooley Crawford's backyard. Annie shucked the fresh roasted corn while her mother, Carleen, set up the Slip 'n Slide for Justin and Delaney.

"You kids put on some sunscreen." Annie waved a tube at them. "Dinner is almost ready."

Already soaked, both kids ran dripping back to the patio, lathered on sunscreen and dashed toward the slide, bare feet slapping the plastic. Their squeals and laughter warmed Annie from the inside out.

Mother lifted the grill lid, flipped the chicken breasts, smoke and scent rolling.

"Smells great, Mom."

"I wonder where your dad is." Her mother lowered the lid and laid the spatula aside. "He should be here by now."

"Give him a call. Tell him he has ten minutes before Justin devours his corn." Annie stripped away the charred husk to get to the perfectly roasted yellow kernels.

"That should get him moving. Be back in a minute." Mother slipped through the patio doors into the house, returning with the cordless in hand and a disappointed expression.

"What?" Annie asked. "Don't tell me Dad's still working."

"Yes. Again." Her mother's voice was tight with annoyance.

"No wonder his ulcer eats him up."

"That's what I tell him. He works too much. He has deputies that could handle things, but he thinks he's the only one who can do it right."

"Dad's way or the highway." She plopped a cleaned ear onto a platter.

"Isn't that the truth?" Carleen tried to smile, but Annie could see how bothered she was by the absence. "He knew you and the kids were coming over. You've been so busy at the Hawkins's place we haven't had a cookout together all summer. He should have made the time."

"I know, but it's okay. Really. I'm used to his absence." From the time she was small, Dad's police work came first. He'd missed more than one of her basketball games as well as her middle school promotion.

Her mother sighed and finished putting the meal on the wrought-iron table. As the four of them ate dinner, Carleen was unusually quiet even though Justin and Delaney were clowning around and pretty funny. When the last corn was crunched and the meal cleared away, Annie thought of why she'd come over in the first place.

"Mom, do you mind if I go through some of the photo albums? I want to find some old pictures."

"Why, no, of course not. You know where they are."

"Come with me." Annie hooked an arm through her mother's. "Maybe looking at those old snapshots will cheer you up."

"Some of them make me laugh, that's for sure."

Leaving the kids to play, they headed inside. Carleen went

to the bedroom and returned with a stack of albums. "Any particular pictures you wanted?"

"Hmm. Yes." Annie prowled through the half-dozen books. "From when I was small up through high school. I'm helping Sloan with a project."

"Oh." Annie knew that tone of voice. Sloan was never a pleasant topic, even with her mother, though Mom was nicer about him than Dad. "What kind of project?"

"A couple, actually. An album for Sloan of his boyhood, to start with. I'm sure there are some of the two of us in here."

"Undoubtedly." Mother and Daddy hadn't minded Annie and Sloan playing together as children, but at some point—probably when they began to date—all that changed. The son of Redemption's worst criminal was not considered good enough for the police chief's daughter.

"I also had the idea of putting together a book of wedding photos taken in the Hawkins's garden. Weren't you and Daddy married there?"

"We were. I have lots of wedding shots. You know how I love capturing special occasions."

They began leafing through the photos, selecting a few to be copied. Annie was glad to see her mother's mood lightening as she told stories about the old snapshots.

"This was when your daddy was first named police chief." Carleen's voice was filled with pride. "He'd worked such long hours to get there. He was the youngest chief in the state at that time."

Annie had heard the story before but didn't mind. She was proud of her father, too. She turned another page. "What's this one? Dad's all dressed up but he doesn't look too happy."

Her mother leaned in for a look. "That was his fortieth birthday. He was so bothered by that number he wouldn't let me throw a party for him, but I bought him that beautiful watch."

The comment drew Annie's attention to her father's out-stretched wrist. "I don't remember him having one like that."

"That's because he lost it that same night. I was already furious with him for going to work instead of letting me take him out to dinner as I'd planned. But duty called."

"As it always does," Annie said wryly, thinking of tonight's cookout.

"Yes. And he was gone half the night. Something about cows on the road or a bull getting hit by a truck. I don't remember. Anyway, he lost that expensive watch and I didn't speak to him for days."

"Mom," Annie admonished.

"Sounds silly now, doesn't it? To be mad at him on his birthday." She flipped a page. "Look here, honey. This one is you and Sloan. You were about Justin's age, I guess. Maybe a little older."

"I remember that. We attended a birthday picnic in the town square." Annie's heart squeezed. She wondered if her mother noticed that Sloan and Justin shared the same lanky frame and the same way of tilting their heads to smile. "He was handsome even then."

"And sad-looking, I thought. This was after Joni ran off. Poor little thing. I couldn't help feeling sorry for him back then."

"I know you did. You were always kind to him." Annie patted her mother's arm. "I asked him to come with me tonight."

"Well, honey, I'm glad he didn't accept. You know how your dad is, especially when it comes to his little girl."

"I'm not a teenager anymore, Mom. I'm a responsible adult. And in case Dad hasn't noticed, so is Sloan. He just lost his aunt. He's terribly alone. Showing kindness and compassion is the Christian thing to do. You taught me that."

"Yes, but Sloan was a wild child, Annie. A troublemaker long before his mother ran off with that trucker. Being kind and getting personally involved are two different things. I just don't trust him after the way he hurt you."

Annie had to admit she struggled with the same issues, but her parents' outright rejection of Sloan because of the past irritated her. "He's changed, Mom. Besides, Sloan was never the terrible person Daddy made him out to be. He was ornery and rebellious, but never violent." A lot like your grandson, she wanted to say. "Toilet-papering the principal's house is not capital murder."

"Vandalism is nothing to take lightly. As you well know from Justin's recent experience."

"I'm not excusing Sloan's behavior. But he was a boy. A boy who thought the whole town hated him because of his parents' mistakes. Besides, did anyone ever bother to ask why he did those things?"

"The principal suspended him for fighting."

"Because a kid called his mother a bad name."

"Excuses don't change the stripes on a tiger."

"The Sloan I knew wasn't perfect—" Her mother made a rude noise but Annie went on. For once, Mother was going to listen to reason. Annie was tired of her parents behaving as if Sloan was Typhoid Mary. "He was also gentle and kind, a champion of the underdog, though no one gave him any credit. If he took up for someone, he was the one who ended up in trouble." Partly because he was too proud to tell the whole story. "I remember once when a bunch of kids were tormenting a poor cat with its head stuck in a salmon can. Instead of joining the crowd, Sloan chased the kids away and spent ten minutes gently freeing the hysterical cat."

"Which is nice if it's true."

"I was there. I know it happened. Just as I know a lot of other good things about Sloan." She gnawed at her lip. "I can't help wondering what would have happened if he'd never left town. He was better to me than any boy I ever dated, including Joey."

Her mother studied her with concerned eyes. "I don't like the sound of your voice, Annie. You be careful. The last thing you need is to fall for him again."

Annie pressed her lips together, and then with a sigh admitted, "I think I already have."

Carleen sat back against the couch cushions, hand against her throat. "Honey, be sensible. That boy has never been good for you. He broke your heart."

"That *boy* is a man. A good man."

"You don't know that. He's been here a couple of months. You don't know what he's been up to for the last ten years."

"Twelve."

Her mother batted the air. "Whatever. The point is you're a lonely divorcée who never had any sense when it came to men."

Cut to the heart, Annie gasped. "Mother!"

"Well, I'm sorry, honey, but it's true. Dad and I have tried to save you from heartache your whole life and you seem to chase it down. When you were a teen, we were frantic with worry over the way you threw yourself at Sloan. If you would have listened to reason in the first place, Dad would never have taken such drastic measures to get him away from you. But no, you wanted the town bad boy and nothing we could say made any difference."

"Wait. Wait." Annie held up both hands, her brain locked on one statement. "Back up. What do you mean Dad had to take drastic measures? I thought Sloan left because he was in trouble." Her heart thumped with a sudden, frightening thought. "Did Daddy do something to make Sloan leave town? Is that what you mean?"

Her mother's face paled. "I— What I mean is— Nothing, just nothing." But she pressed fingers against each temple as if a headache threatened and Annie knew. She *knew* her mother was hiding something.

Her throat went dry. "Mother, tell me what you're talking about. *Tell me.*"

Carleen swung her body away, fist pressed against her mouth. "I shouldn't have said anything."

"But you did and now I have to know. Did Daddy do something to make Sloan leave? Was there more to the burglary charge than I know about?"

Her mother took a shaky breath. "Your daddy was beside himself with worry. He was scared his little girl was getting too involved with the wrong boy and he had to do something."

"What kind of something?" Annie's voice rose. Certain her heart was going to explode, she pressed the photo albums against her chest.

"Please don't tell your daddy I told you this. There was no burglary."

Annie's mouth dropped open. "Sloan was innocent?"

"Yes." Carleen's hands twisted in her lap. She looked away, unable to meet Annie's eyes. "Don't hate us, honey. We did what we thought was best for our child. You're a parent. You understand that."

Did what? What did they do? Annie's brain reeled with the implications, most of which still made no sense. "I don't understand. If Sloan knew he was innocent, why did he leave?"

"I told you, the charge wasn't burglary."

"What was it?" What crime was so terrible that Sloan would leave and never look back?

Head down, Mother's answer was a tired whisper. "Rape."

"Rape?" Annie nearly shouted. "Of who?"

Carleen's expression was haunted as she turned to her daughter. "You."

Chapter Fourteen

Annie couldn't breathe. She was smothering. Absolutely smothering. Desperate, she rolled down the window of her car, cranked the A/C full blast and drove faster.

This was unreal. It could not be happening. Sloan had been accused of raping her?

A hysterical giggle erupted, completely out of line with what was going on inside her body. Nausea rolled through her. Sweat beaded on her face and neck.

Lies. Deceit. Ruined lives. Mother and Daddy had no idea the twisted set of circumstances they'd set into motion on prom night twelve years ago.

Why hadn't Sloan told her the truth? Why had he run away instead of facing the false accusation?

She turned down the lane toward the Hawkins's house, gravel spewing out behind. She slammed on the brakes and was out of the car before it stopped rocking.

"Sloan!" she cried. Her feet hit the porch running.

The door opened and Sloan was there.

"Annie, what's wrong?" Sloan gripped her shoulders, blue

eyes wide with concern. "The kids? Where are the kids? What's happened?"

The sheer panic in his voice calmed her. He was worried about her kids. Dear Lord, she loved him so much. How could this have happened? "At Mother's. They're fine. It's not them. It's you."

"Me?" He blinked in confusion, worry lines deepening. "I'm fine, but you're shaking all over. Come inside out of the heat and tell me what's going on."

Sloan slid an arm around her waist and gently drew her inside. Gratefully, Annie leaned into him, afraid her knees wouldn't hold her much longer.

"Sit," he commanded. "I'll get you some water."

Numbly, she slumped onto the couch and wrapped her arms around her waist. Her stomach hurt. Her heart hurt. Oh, what had her parents done to her—and to this good man?

Sloan returned with a glass of ice water and crouched in front of her. "Drink this."

She could feel him watching her while she gulped half the contents, letting the cold calm the fire in her belly. When she finished, he took the glass and set it aside.

"What happened? Are you all right?" He balanced on his toes in front of her, watchful.

"Mother told me something tonight." Annie took a breath that didn't quite satisfy the air hunger. She felt as if she'd been punched and no amount of breathing would ever again be enough. "She didn't intend to but she did."

"What kind of something?"

"About you, about prom night twelve years ago."

Sloan went still. "Yeah?"

"She said Dad accused you of rape."

A beat of silence and then the cautious reply. "Now you know."

She searched his face. He was still hiding something. But

what? "Stop hedging, Sloan. You were accused of raping me. And we both know that's a lie."

He looked toward the ceiling, then pushed to a stand and turned his back. "She shouldn't have told you. I didn't want you to know."

"Why? Why, Sloan?" Annie grabbed his arm and pulled him around. "I would have testified on your behalf no matter what my parents thought. Why didn't you give me the chance to defend you?"

Sloan rubbed his hands down his face. "Think about what you just said, Annie. Think about it. If I had stayed to fight, everyone in town would have known about the charges. The gossips like Roberta Prine would have gone wild. You were a nice girl. I couldn't do that to you."

"I don't understand—" But suddenly comprehension flooded her. "Oh, Sloan. My wonderful Sloan. You left to protect my reputation, didn't you?"

Expression hard and controlled, he nodded. "If I'd known you were pregnant, nothing and no one could have made me leave. But your dad knew he had an ace in the hole. He knew I loved you enough to protect you if I could. He tossed the options on the table and I saw no choice but to do as he demanded."

Slowly, Annie rose from the sofa. Years of self-doubt fell away as she touched Sloan's face.

"You loved me that much." Sloan hadn't abandoned her. He'd left to protect her, and he'd gone on protecting her with his silence until today.

"I did." His throat worked for a moment before he said, "Still do."

The tragic beauty of his sacrifice welled inside her until tears of grief and regret broke free. "All this time, I wondered what I had done to drive you away."

"Oh, Annie girl, don't cry. You never did anything. Don't

you know that? Not one thing other than give me hope."
Tenderly, he drew her to him until she was cradled against his
broad chest. Tears rolled over her cheeks and onto his shirt-
front as she let go of twelve years of self-doubt and heartache.
Sloan loved her. He always had.

Emotion boiled inside Sloan like hot lava. Seeing Annie
cry tore him apart. At the same time, a load lifted from his
shoulders. Annie knew the truth. He'd never wanted her hurt
that way, especially with all the events that had been set into
motion that long ago night. He wondered if Dooley would
have gone ahead with his plan to get rid of the town bad boy
if he'd known Annie was pregnant? Probably. The chief would
have wanted him gone even more.

Part of him wanted to rip Dooley's head off and make him
pay for the harm he'd inflicted. But another part of him knew
he wouldn't be the man he was today if he hadn't been forced
into the military. Aunt Lydia hadn't known the truth any more
than Annie had, but she'd always told him God had a way of
working things out. Sloan only wished the plan hadn't been
so hard on Annie.

With a sigh, he kissed the top of her soft hair and smoothed
aside the tickling strands. What a tangled mess he'd unwit-
tingly left behind.

"I'm sorry, pretty girl, for all the hurt I've ever caused you."

A soft rustling sound came as she shook her head against
his shirt front. "Not your fault. You were hurt, too. Daddy did
this to both of us."

She pulled back a little to look up at him. Her eyes were
red and puffy and Sloan could no more keep from touching
his lips to each one than he could bring his Aunt Lydia back
from Heaven. He had loved this woman for so long. She had
no idea the power she held over him.

His heart thundered in his chest. After all the water that flowed under Redemption Bridge, was there a chance he and Annie could start again? Now that the cat was out of the bag, what did they have to lose?

But he knew the answer before he asked. Dooley would always stand in the way. Annie loved her dad, and though Sloan despised his tactics, Dooley apparently wanted only the best for his daughter. So did Sloan.

Sloan had had so little of family in his own life he knew the value of relationships. Expecting Annie to choose was unfair. "I don't want to come between you and your family."

The corner of her mouth curved. "You always have."

Sloan gave a short laugh. "Ah, Annie. What are we going to do now?"

She laid a palm against his cheek, soothing him as she'd done when he was a wild and angry boy. His eyes fell shut and he soaked her into his soul. Somehow, some way, he would make peace with Dooley Crawford for the sake of the woman they both loved.

Chapter Fifteen

A long time later, subdued and emotionally rent, Sloan and Annie sat side by side on the sofa talking and leafing through the photo albums Annie had inadvertently brought along. For now, peace flowed between them and the sweet joy of shared love.

She'd not said the words, but Annie loved him. Her love was in everything she did, as it had always been. Annie nurtured his broken soul with her smiles and gentle words.

His throat ached with loving her and with gratitude to God for bringing them to this moment. Maybe, God willing, they could make things work out, and he could be the father to his son and to Delaney that he had never had.

The idea scared him, but he would not let fear interfere with his life anymore. For it was fear he now knew that had kept him away from Redemption. Fear that Annie hated him. Fear that he would once again become the pathetic, despised bad seed of the murderer Clayton Hawkins and a woman who would abandon her child in the dark of night.

Annie was bent forward, her blond hair sweeping along her beautiful cheekbones, perusing the photos. Sloan tenderly brushed her hair behind one ear. She turned with a curious smile and his heart flip-flopped.

"Find anything interesting?" he asked. She'd shown him pictures of the two of them together and they'd laughed at their funny hairstyles. Nostalgia rolled through him, bittersweet. All his memories of Redemption were not bad after all.

Annie tapped a snapshot. "Mother took this at Amy Childers's birthday party. Remember? You won the prize for spinning a basketball on your finger the longest."

Sloan chuckled at the skinny youth. "Look at those muscles."

"Scrawny like Justin."

Annie flipped a page and a photo caught Sloan's attention. He frowned and leaned forward, all frivolity disappearing. "What's that?"

"What's what? Oh, that picture of Daddy? His fortieth birthday, Mom said. I don't remember it either."

"No, not the picture. That." Sloan's pulse started to race. He put a finger on Dooley Crawford's wrist.

"A watch Mom bought him for his birthday. Why?"

Flashes of memory flickered through Sloan's head. Memories of the last time he'd seen his mother.

"No reason." Sloan began to shake inside. If Annie knew the suspicions dancing through his brain, she'd walk out and never look back. "Does your dad still have that watch?"

"Mom said he lost it that same night. She was really upset with him."

Suddenly, other things began to click into place. The dark, creased pants, the blue dress shirt, a man who didn't fit the description of Mama's usual drunken guest. And most importantly, the fancy turquoise bracelet with silver sunbursts.

Sloan squinted at the date on the photo. Alarms went off in his head. Dooley's birthday matched the date of his mother's disappearance. Coincidence? By itself, maybe. Coupled with the turquoise watch? No way.

"I thought it was a bracelet," he murmured, finger tracing the telltale piece of jewelry. "But it was a watch."

The man he'd seen through the crack in the door had not been a trucker who lured Mama away. Her visitor had been Dooley Crawford. Something was rotten in the Redemption Police Department.

"Sloan?" Annie sat back to gaze at him. "What are you talking about? Is there something about Daddy's watch?"

Could the police chief possibly know more about his mother's disappearance than he'd let on? Could he have done to Joni Hawkins what he'd done, years later, to her son?

There was only one way to find out.

Sloan yanked to a stand. "I have to go somewhere."

"Where? Sloan, what's going on? You look like a thunderstorm about to break."

Maybe he was. "I need to talk to your dad about something."

"About us? Sloan, don't. You'll only end up in trouble. Please don't go."

"I have to." Afraid she'd stop him if he lingered, Sloan grabbed his keys and stalked out the door to his Harley. Annie followed, her frightened voice pleading with him to wait.

But he couldn't. Too many years had passed while Dooley kept his secrets.

Tonight, Redemption's police chief had some explaining to do.

The motorcycle skidded sideways as Sloan downshifted onto the gravel road leading to Dooley Crawford's farmland. He'd stopped at the police station only to hear that the chief had left. According to Deputy Rainmaker, the chief usually drove out to check on his cattle before heading home. The locale suited Sloan just fine. He wasn't crazy about confronting the man in front of his wife, so this was better, and he knew the way to the Crawford farm. As kids, he and Annie had fished the pond and picked their fill of wild blackberries.

The iron gate was unlocked, and Sloan felt a sense of satisfaction at knowing he'd discovered Dooley's whereabouts. A hay barn sat beyond the pond in a stand of trees, a barn he and Annie had discovered as teenagers. He regretted that now. She'd deserved more respect than he'd shown.

The police chief's pickup truck was parked near the pond and twenty or thirty head of red Hereford cattle milled around. Sloan revved the Harley to make his presence known.

Dooley looked up. Even from this distance, Sloan knew he'd been recognized. The chief tossed a feed sack into the back of his truck and dusted his hands down his pantlegs before taking a wide, defensive stance.

No point pretending they liked each other.

Sloan parked the bike and walked across the dry, browning grass, fists tight at his sides.

God, help me do this right. I don't want to hurt Annie.

All he wanted was information about his mother.

When he was close enough to watch Dooley's face, he said, "What do you know about my mother's disappearance?"

The question shocked the chief. No doubt about it. He blinked, eyes widening. "What are you talking about?"

"You were at our house the night she disappeared."

"You're crazy."

Sloan gave a cocky laugh he didn't feel. "Keep that in mind while we have this friendly little chat."

Dooley's face hardened. "Get off my property."

"Can't do it, Dooley. You're going to tell me what you know. Why were you there? Don't deny it. I saw you. I didn't realize then but I do now."

Crawford's chest expanded in an attempt to intimidate. "Get moving, *boy,* or I'm going to put you in jail where you belong. Just like your rotten-to-the-core daddy."

Twelve years ago, the statement would have been fighting words, and Sloan would have lost his cool and consequently, the battle. Dooley didn't know it, but he wasn't dealing with an undisciplined teenager anymore. "We're talking about you, not me. What were you doing at my house that night?"

"You were a kid. You can't possibly remember."

"I remember a fancy turquoise-and-silver watch on a man's wrist, an expensive watch you don't see very often. You owned that watch the day my mother disappeared. Your fortieth birthday."

Dooley blanched but didn't back down. "I told you to get off my property and I mean it."

"If I leave, I ride straight to the county seat and the D.A.'s office with what I know."

"Jim Watson is a friend. He'll laugh you out of town."

Sloan shrugged, though he was feeling anything but nonchalant. "If he doesn't listen, the OSBI will. You owned that watch. I saw it. I saw *you.* You were there, but for some interesting reason, you never mentioned that in the reports. You told everyone my mother must have left with a trucker. Now that I think about it, where did you get that information? No one else remembers seeing Mama with a man that night."

"There *was* a trucker, you little snot nose." Dooley's face mottled dark red. The chief was getting mad, and in Sloan's experience, angry men made mistakes. "There were always truckers and bums and no-accounts like your daddy in Joni's life."

Sloan tried not to take offense, but protecting his mother's memory was habit. "She wasn't like that, Dooley."

"Sure she was. Men dragged into that little house all hours of the night, but Joni wouldn't give a decent man the time of day."

Something in the chief's tone tickled a memory. Had he heard Dooley say those words to his mother? Had there been something going on between his mother and the chief?

The notion turned Sloan's stomach, but he wasn't about to back off now that he knew he was on the right track.

"A decent man? Like you?"

The chief turned aside and spit, but Sloan could see he was rattled. "Shut up. You don't know anything."

I do now. Grim satisfaction seeped into Sloan's pores. "You were there. I have evidence."

Dooley frowned, nerves twitching. Sloan had struck a nerve. "What kind of evidence?"

Very little. The memory of a child, a watch, and strong suspicion. "Enough to have everyone in Redemption wondering why their elected official covered up a woman's disappearance and then, years later, lied to run her son out of town." When Dooley's furious gaze jerked to meet his, Sloan knew he was right. "Something real fishy about that."

"All right, I was there. Are you satisfied now? But that doesn't prove anything."

Sloan's mouth went dry. His insides churned, wanting to be wrong and knowing he wasn't. "You had a thing for my mother, didn't you?"

Teeth tight, Dooley looked ready to throttle him. "A thing?" he ground out. "Like the thing you had for my daughter?"

The sickness in Sloan's belly exacerbated. He gazed toward the horizon where the dying rays of the sun bled into the sky. Annie's father and Joni?

Lord, what have I uncovered?

The ugly possibilities pushed at his brain. Sloan wished

he'd never started this in the first place. But he had, and for the love of his mother, he had to finish it.

He dragged his gaze back to Dooley. The police chief pointed a revolver straight at his chest.

Chapter Sixteen

"You couldn't leave well enough alone, could you, Hawkins?"

Sloan raised one hand slowly. "Be cool, Crawford. Don't do anything you'll regret."

"The only thing I regret is not sending you with your mother that night." His finger danced around the trigger, threatening. "Get your hands in the air. I don't trust you as far as I can throw that pickup truck."

Focus locked on the pistol—a 9 mm automatic—Sloan slowly raised his hands. "Where? Just tell me where my mother is, and I'll keep the rest quiet."

"You want to know where she is?" A sneer pulled his lips apart in a grotesque smile. He motioned with the gun. "Start walking."

Sloan blinked. "Walk where?"

Dooley motioned again, this time toward the barn. "Move it. And keep your hands up where I can see them. No monkey business."

Doing as he was told, Sloan walked the short distance to the barn, hopes sinking like the sun. All the while his mind raced with a mix of questions about his mother and concern for his own safety. He'd been in tight fixes before, but this might be the worst, and he'd walked right into it like a man who didn't know the first thing about self-protection. Some security expert he was.

When they reached the barn, Dooley said, "Open it and go inside."

Sloan hesitated, searching for escape. Once inside that barn, he'd be at Dooley's mercy. The chief shoved the gun against Sloan's temple. "Open the door, or die now."

Seeing no other choice, Sloan unbolted the latch and went inside the dim barn with the chief close behind. Scents of hay and feed filled his nostrils. His gaze roamed around the structure in search of a weapon. On the opposite wall farm tools dangled too far away to reach.

"Before you kill me, at least tell me where my mother is."

Dooley cackled. Spittle formed at the corners of his mouth. "Might as well tell you, Hawkins. She's right here where I can keep a close eye on her, and you're going to join her."

The horror of Dooley's meaning slithered through him like snake venom. Some part of him had always known Joni would not willingly leave him, but he'd always hoped she was alive and well in some other state. Now he knew, and the knowing was every bit as bad as the not knowing. His arms fell to his sides. "You killed her."

"No. No. You have it all wrong. I never meant for her to get hurt. I swear it on her grave." Dooley waved the gun. "Get your hands in the air!"

Sloan jerked his arms up as he swallowed the bile rising in his throat. "She's buried here?"

"Right there." He pointed the barrel of the pistol toward a concrete slab. "Right there where I could take care of her."

Sloan slumped on to a hay bale and put his head in his hands. He didn't care if Dooley shot him here and now. His

mother was dead. Annie's father had killed his mother. Joni
had never left Redemption at all. And now, Dooley planned
to kill Joni's son.

"Why?" The question was a choked whisper. "What did
she ever do to you?"

"Nothing. Don't you understand anything, boy? Joni and her
men, dozens of them coming and going in her house, sleeping
on her couch. She swore nothing was going on, but I'm a man.
I knew better." His nostrils flared with disgust. "Year after
year, I begged her to be with me, and she turned me down. Me.
A respected man of the community. She'd take in her drunks
and truckers, but Police Chief Dooley was left out in the cold."

Shaking inside, Sloan raised his head to glare at his
mother's murderer. "What about your wife and family,
Dooley? Didn't they matter?"

"You sound like Joni. I got tired of her using my marriage
as an excuse. I was crazy about her. I bought her things but
she refused to take them. I even offered money, but she
returned anything except the tips I left for pie and coffee.
Hundred-dollar tips. For the kid, I'd tell her. Did you know
that? I paid for your fancy basketball shoes."

Sloan shook his head, sick. The man had been obsessed
with a woman he couldn't have. "What happened that night?
What happened to my mother?"

"Might as well tell you. You're not leaving here anyway."
Dooley patted his pocket, removed a roll of antacids and
thumbed one into his mouth, all the while holding the 9 mm
steady. "It was my birthday. Forty years old and miserable.
Carleen wanted to throw a big party and after I flat-out refused
she bought me that watch. I hated it. The only gift I wanted
was Joni. Carleen thought I had to work, but I needed to be
with Joni. Just that one night. Surely, I thought, she'd let me
stay with her. It was my birthday. She owed me that much."

"I heard you talking. Both of you."

As if suddenly aware of Sloan's presence, Dooley jerked the gun higher. "Shut up. This is all your fault. Always was."

"How do you figure?"

"I heard what she said to you, too." Dooley sneered. "You came to the door, whining, wanting to know who was with her. 'Nobody important,' she said." His voice took on a snide tone, imitating Joni's insult. "Me. The man who loved her more than anyone else, was 'nobody important.'"

Stall, Sloan. Stall for time. Somehow, some way, he had to keep Dooley talking until he could figure a way out of this mess. "Guess that made you pretty mad."

"Furious. We argued. I begged her. A man like me begging a woman like that." He jabbed the gun at Sloan. "Do you know how humiliating that is to a man of my position?"

"So you killed her?"

"No!" Dooley kicked out, striking Sloan in the shin. Sloan grunted, reflexively bending to rub the offended leg. "Get your hands up in the air like I told you. Stupid boy never listened. I only wanted to kiss her, to apologize, to show her how much she meant to me, but when I put my arms around her, she went crazy."

Dooley turned to pace, apparently reliving the awful moment. Sloan desperately searched his surroundings. If he dove for Dooley's knees and knocked him off balance, he might be able to get control of the weapon. He tensed, ready to pounce, but before he could act, Dooley stopped and spun. "Don't even think about it, Hawkins. You'd be dead before you could take your next breath."

"You're going to kill me anyway."

Dooley chuckled. "True. A pleasure, I might add. Strange to love the mother and hate the son, but there you go. You were always her first concern. Always the one she promised to

spend time with. I followed the pair of you sometimes.
watched her with you."

The police chief was a sick man.

"How did my mother die? At least tell me that."

"Why should I? Maybe I'll let you die never knowing."

"You won't get away with killing me."

"I got away with Joni's, didn't I? Everyone believed me

"You started the rumor?"

"Of course." He seemed proud. "And the town bought
easily. Running off with a trucker fit Joni's lifestyle, just a
your disappearance will be accepted. You ran off before whe
trouble came. You're going to do it again. No one will eve
know you're buried in that corner next to your mother. I'll ad
another concrete stall for birthing calves and no one will b
the wiser. A dead body is a simple thing for a police chief t
dispose of."

Sloan's blood ran cold. This man had disposed of hi
mother's body here in this very barn. His mama, the woma
who'd soothed his nightmares and bandaged his skinne
knees, had ended her days in a barn. He shook with loathing
"So, her death was accidental?"

"Of course it was an accident. I told you. She fell. I ju
wanted to kiss her, but she fought me like a tiger. Broke m
new watch. Next thing I know she's on the floor, her hea
bleeding, her neck at an odd angle. I didn't kill her." He leane
toward Sloan, voice rising to a shout. "She fell. Understand
I *did not* kill her." Using the gun hand, Dooley wiped the sid
of a shaky hand over his eyes. Sloan started to make his move

Dooley leveled the gun at his face and the chance was los
"Enough talk. Get up. You got a grave to dig."

Annie shook so hard she was weak. Hands pressed to he
mouth to keep from crying out, she gazed at the two deputie

tanding on either side of the barn. One—Jessie Rainmaker—
ave a headshake and held a finger to his lips.

When Sloan had burst out the door with fire in his eyes,
he'd known something terrible was going to happen, but not
his. Not the admission by her father that he'd killed Sloan's
mother. The horror of that truth was too much to bear. Her
ather was a murderer.

And Sloan was in danger.

Oh, Lord, Oh, Lord, please help us. I'm so scared.

Chest rising and falling fast enough to hyperventilate, she
istened with every fiber of her being to the conversation
going on inside the barn. The deputies listened, too, expres-
ions tight with shock. They'd come, thinking to protect their
oss, and now this. They must be as heartsick as she.

"What about my bike, Dooley?" Sloan's voice penetrated
he metal door. "A Harley is hard to hide."

"Shut up and keep digging. I gotta think."

"Want a suggestion?" He sounded calm, almost arrogant,
ut he had to be scared. That was her Sloan, cool on the
outside, boiling on the inside.

"What? Don't try anything with me, Hawkins. I'll gut
hoot you and bury you alive."

The statement curled Annie's toes. That was her father
alking. The man who'd bought her a pony and taught her to
wim.

Oh, God in Heaven, help us. This can't be real.

"Bring the Harley inside. Bury it with me."

Annie jerked. How could Sloan make such a macabre suggestion? Her gaze flew to Deputy Rainmaker. Though his
ace was grim and shocked, he winked and motioned for her
o go back to the car. She shook her head. She couldn't leave.
Not with the two men she loved most in the world locked in
a battle of life or death.

The deputy bared his teeth, jerked his head and mouthed "Go!"

He was right. She endangered them all by staying. On wobbly legs, she crept away, careful not to make a sound. All the while, she flung half-baked prayers toward Heaven. Save Sloan. Save her father. *Oh, God, help.*

Her father was a murderer.

When she reached the far corner of the barn, away from the entrance, Annie folded double, hands tight on her belly. Her daddy had killed Joni Hawkins and buried her body under this very building. Poor Sloan. Her father had been responsible for all those lonely, heartbroken years Sloan had endured as a child. He was responsible, too, for Sloan's exile. Lies and deceit and cover-up. Her own father.

Suddenly, the barn door opened and Sloan stepped out, hands in the air. From where she hid, she could only see his back. Then her father stepped out, holding a gun to Sloan's head. She knew the moment he spotted the two deputies. All the starch went out of him.

Annie caught snatches of conversation.

"Put it down, Chief. No need for anyone to get hurt."

"Jessie, am I glad to see you." Unaware that they'd been listening for a long time, the police chief seemed determined to keep up the charade. "Put this man under arrest."

"What's the charge?" Deputy Rainmaker's expression was a mix of wanting to believe his boss and knowing the hard facts.

"Breaking and entering, assault with a deadly weapon. He tried to kill me with a shovel. Threatened to bury me in my own barn."

The other deputy stepped up beside her father. "Let me have the gun, Dooley. I'll take it from here. We heard everything."

"What do you mean? What did you hear? Hawkins threat-

ning me?" When both deputies just stared at him with sad
xpressions, he stopped blustering. Looking bewildered and
ien beaten, he lowered his weapon. Deputy Rainmaker
vrenched it from his grasp.

"Chief, I have to read you your rights."

And that's when Annie slipped away to the waiting police
ar. She couldn't listen any longer. Her father was a criminal.
verything bad in Sloan's life could be traced back to
)ooley Crawford.

The jubilant hope that she and Sloan could finally be together
ided with the daylight. She would always be a reminder of the
ian who'd killed his mother. Her family had caused all the
eartache in his life. Why would he want her now? The best
ling she could do for Sloan was to leave him alone.

Sloan watched in despair as Chief Dooley Crawford was
oaded into the back of a police car next to his sobbing
aughter. According to the deputies, Annie had come to them,
fraid of a showdown between the police chief and Sloan.
he'd been right. And now she'd be shattered.

On legs of rubber, Sloan started toward the car, relieved to
e alive and yet heartsick at what the night had revealed. He
eeded to hold Annie, to comfort them both and explain the
nexplainable. He'd come to the farm for answers, with no
lea of the deceit and death he would uncover. He hadn't
ome to cause Dooley's downfall. But he had.

All he'd ever done was bring Annie unhappiness.

The police car's engine roared to life. Sloan picked up his
ace. The deputy put the transmission into gear. The cruiser
iade a slow circle to turn around and as Annie's window
ame into his line of vision, their eyes met for one brief,
ainful moment.

"Annie," he said.

Then her face crumpled and she turned away and left him standing in the dust...alone.

Chapter Seventeen

The next three days were torture.

The news about Police Chief Dooley Crawford broke and Sloan spent hours at the police station giving his deposition. People called him on the telephone and dropped by the house. Finally, today, except for the authorities he was forced to see, he answered neither the phone nor the door. The only person he wanted to hear from was Annie and she was nowhere to be seen. He considered going to her, but figured he'd hurt her enough. Even if she didn't hate him, Sloan loved her enough to get out of her life and stop causing so many problems.

He tossed a handful of socks into his duffel bag.

The garden wasn't finished. He regretted that. But this morning he'd put the house on the market. The buyer could finish the work and hopefully follow through with the aborted plans he and Annie had made to reopen the garden for weddings.

He'd have to come back eventually for the trial, a trip that would kill him if he had to face Annie across a courtroom. There was also talk of exhuming his mother's remains. The idea filled him with dread. Joni Hawkins had been through enough, but he supposed an autopsy was necessary to make the charges against Dooley stick. And she deserved a proper burial.

He scrubbed his hands up and down his face, exhausted but unable to sleep. He'd prayed a lot over the last few days, but his prayers had bounced off the ceiling. He didn't even know what to pray for.

After zipping the duffel bag, he tossed it over his shoulder and started down the stairs for one last walk-through to make sure the windows were secure before turning the key over to the Realtor.

He dropped the duffel at the foot of the stairs and went from room to room. Outside the garden room, he paused. Notches and dates lined the doorframe where Lydia had measured his height every year on his birthday. Clayton Hawkins's measurements were there, too, a silent reminder of the Hawkins blood running through his veins.

With a sigh, Sloan trailed his fingers over the notches one last time. The garden room was empty now, free of Lydia's makeshift bedroom, but no longer the sunny, white wicker room filled with plants he remembered from boyhood.

So many questions had been answered since his return. Yet Sloan Hawkins was as alone as ever.

No, that wasn't true. He had God now and a peace inside no matter how much he hurt with all that had happened.

Movement caught the corner of his eye and he looked out the window.

Someone was in the garden. A lanky figure wandered aimlessly through the colorful flower beds.

His chest squeezed. Justin.

What was he going to do about his son? Would Annie let him have any part at all in the boy's life now? Or would Justin be as lost to him as his mother and Annie?

With heavy heart and unsure of what he would say to the son that wasn't his to claim, Sloan slid open the French doors and stepped out onto the veranda.

A hot wind came around the corner of the house. Instant sweat this time of year.

He stood, one hand on the veranda railing, watching his son, loving him and helpless to do anything about it. Justin must have felt his stare, for he looked over one shoulder.

"Hey," Sloan said.

Justin's nostrils flared. "You're a jerk."

"Yeah. I know. I'm sorry."

"Save it for someone who cares."

Well, so much for a friendly father-son conversation. He stepped off the porch and started toward the boy. "You okay?"

"You tell me. My grandpa is in jail for murdering my grandma. My other grandma is knocked out on nerve medicine. My mom won't stop crying and now my dad is leaving." He jutted a belligerent chin. "You *are* leaving, aren't you? Walking out. Just like my old man. Dads are jerks."

"Look, Justin, you don't understand. Life is complicated sometimes. I never—"

"Save the bull. I understand plenty. You show up like some big shot on a Harley and make my mama happy again and now you're making her cry."

"What are you talking about?" Annie was crying over her father, not him.

"Don't play dumb. You know what you did."

"I never meant to cause your mother any harm. Your grandfather either."

"Yeah, well, Grandpa is a jerk, too." Tears welled in the boy's eyes. Sloan could see the emotion infuriated him. "He killed your mom, he should pay for it. That's what he told me when I got into trouble. Do the crime, you do the time."

Sloan couldn't argue that, but he didn't want Justin suffering for his grandfather's sins. "None of this has anything to do with you."

"Sure it does." His shoulder twitched. "But I already know none of it is my fault, so don't go Dr. Phil on me, okay?"

Sloan almost smiled. Chip off the old block. He loved this kid. If he had nothing else in life to be thankful for, he'd celebrate the son he hadn't known.

Justin picked up a dirt clod and chucked it against the fence. "Will you talk to Mom before you leave?"

"Better not."

"Figures. Jerk." Another dirt clod slammed the fence.

Sloan sighed and reached down for his own dirt clod. "Understand something, son, I love your mother, but all I've ever done is hurt her."

"Yeah, like now when you're walking out on her again. I heard her talking to Jilly this morning. You know Jilly, Mom's friend." When Sloan nodded in recognition, the boy continued. "She started crying and Jilly said she should talk to you about something."

"About what?"

"I don't know. When Mom was crying she said some dumb, mushy stuff about real love being forever." He chucked another clod and then spun on his tennis shoes. "What's the use? Go back to Virginia. I don't care. Mom will get over you. We all will."

Before Justin reached the freshly painted picket gate his words clicked inside Sloan's brain. *Real love was forever.* Did that mean Annie loved him enough to put aside all the grief and heartache between them?

Was it possible she didn't blame him for her father's fall from grace?

He let the dirt ball fall to the ground at his feet. One thing was for sure, he was not leaving town without talking things over with Annie. He'd done that before and missed years of Justin's life. If Annie wanted him gone, she'd have to tell him to his face.

"Hey, Justin."

The boy paused, one hand on the gate. "What?"

"Want a ride on my bike?"

"Where?"

"To your house. I need to talk to your mother."

Annie thought she might go ahead and have that heart attack she'd been promising herself when she heard the roar of a Harley and saw her son on the seat behind Sloan.

"I want to ride, too."

Annie looked down at Delaney. "Don't even ask."

"But why? Justin got a ride."

Ignoring the common refrain, Annie burst out the front door and into the yard. "What do you think you're doing?"

Simultaneously, father and son dismounted the bike and exchanged grins. Justin unfastened the chin strap on a helmet Annie had never seen before. Did Sloan actually own a helmet?

"I told you she'd be mad."

"Worried, not mad," Annie corrected.

Justin had never been impressed with her worry. "I had to talk to Sloan."

"About?"

Sloan motioned toward the house. "We need to talk. You and me."

Annie's heart skipped a beat. "We do?"

"I'm not leaving until we've cleared the air."

But he *was* leaving. Why did the announcement hurt so badly when she'd prepared for this moment? "Justin, you and

Delaney go play in your rooms for a little while. Sloan and I need some privacy."

Justin cast another glance at Sloan before taking Delaney's hand. "Come on, I'll play that dolly game with you."

Delaney's face scrunched up. "You hate that game."

"Yeah, I know. Come on. Grown-up talk is important."

The kids disappeared inside and Annie waited, awkward and uncertain.

Sloan motioned toward the house again. "Mind if we talk inside?"

"Oh, sure." She led the way, painfully aware of Sloan close at her back. If he touched her, she'd crumble. Afraid she'd plead with him to stay in this town he hated, Annie took a seat across the room.

Instead of sitting in the indicated chair, Sloan paced. He said nothing for the longest time. Finally, he cleared his throat. "I'm sorry about your dad. In my wildest dreams, I never suspected he was the man I'd seen the night my mother disappeared."

"You must hate him."

"I'm trying not to. A year ago, I would have. Now—" He shrugged. "Hate is counterproductive. If I love you, I can't hate your father."

Unable to believe her ears, Annie slowly rose. "Did you just say you love me? After everything my father has done to destroy you?"

"Real love is forever." His words were spoken with a soft, hopeful smile. "Isn't that what you told Jilly?"

Embarrassment heated her cheeks. Justin and his big ears. "I— Sloan, don't feel obligated."

He covered the floor between them in two giant strides. "Obligated? Annie girl, you are my heart and soul. I'm the problem. Always have been. I've caused you nothing but trouble, enough to make you throw me under a bus, though I never meant to." He thumped a fist against his chest. "I can't breathe when I think about never seeing you again."

Annie blinked twice and then still couldn't believe what she'd just heard. "You think the blame was yours? You think I'd hold my father's sins against you?"

"Don't you?" His jaw worked and it was all she could do not to throw her arms around him.

"No! Nothing that's happened is your fault. Or mine either. Listen to me and listen good, Sloan Hawkins. Even if you leave and never come back, you take my love with you. Again."

With a groan that pierced Annie to the soul, Sloan yanked her against his chest. She went willingly, happily, and circled her arms around him, feeling the powerful thud of his heart against hers.

"I can't go. I can't. I tried to do what was best for you, but—" His desperate mouth found her hair, her ear, her cheek.

Flushed, thrilled, her heart banging out of her ribcage, Annie reveled in his touch. Finally. *Finally.*

"I was afraid," she whispered, turning her face toward his.

"Me, too," he murmured against her lips. "Terrified."

"Never again. We have to trust each other."

"Always. Forever." He pulled back a little. "Marry me, Annie. Marry me in the garden our son and this town helped restore." His fingers played across her cheek. "What do you say, pretty girl? Wanna grow old together?"

"What about your business?"

"You are my business. You and Justin and Delaney. The job in Virginia is something I can do anywhere in the world. A little travel, maybe, but I'll take you with me. We'll see the world together."

"I'd love that." Was this happening? But the look in Sloan's eyes told her it was.

Fingers rough but tender, he caressed her cheek, his intense blue gaze holding hers. "Every time I took a trip, I'd think of how much better it would be if you were there. I want to show you everything. To give you everything."

Happiness curved the corners of her mouth. Oh, how she loved this man. "Sounds like bribery."

He squinted at her. "Is it working? Will you be my love, my wife, my heart forever after?"

Relishing the moment, basking in the glow of love finally realized, Annie caressed the soft hair at the nape of his neck. He had wonderful hair. Wonderful eyes. A wonderful heart. "On one condition."

He nipped at her lips. "I like negotiations. What's the condition?"

"I want to live with you in that wonderful old Victorian, to raise our children there, to make new and beautiful memories that will cover all the bad ones."

Sloan leaned his forehead against hers and sighed. "See why I love you? You always say the right things."

"I love that house. Your roots are there. Justin's, too. Years of good, solid people named Hawkins."

"Yeah." Wonder lit his blue, blue eyes. He smiled and Annie knew he finally understood who he was.

"I love you, Sloan Hawkins, daddy to my son, love of my life, good and decent man of honor."

His face softened, tender and emotional. "Oh, Annie. My sweet, sweet Annie."

Then she pulled him close and rocked them back and forth, content and filled. For finally and at last, the fog had cleared, the past was behind them and they could move forward to the future.

Epilogue

The Redemption Register proclaimed it the wedding of the century when early in October, Sloan Hawkins wed Annie Markham in the newly renovated Wedding Garden. Annie found the exaggeration endearing but agreed, as she glanced out the window of the garden room to the gathering throng, it was, by far, one of the best days of her life.

The weather was perfect, as if it had no choice, and only the slightest breeze with a hint of cool ruffled the glorious flood of color. Guests flowed in through the open picket gate which had been appropriately decorated in a cheerful spray of bow-tied sunflowers. The stately Victorian home, the residence of generations of Hawkinses, was alive with laughter and antic-ipation, as it was always meant to be. In celebration of the day, the season and the reopening of the Wedding Garden, apricot-colored tulle dotted with mums in splashes of orange, yellow and bronze festooned the wrap-around veranda. The tulle repeated in dips and swirls down the steps, into the garden and as a border along either side of the leaf-strewn pathway leading to the lush green meadow at the far end. There, a wedding arbor twined with tulle and ivy was bracketed by white guest chairs and shaded by showy red and gold maples. Beneath that arbor, she would join her life to Sloan's.

Delighted butterflies took flight in her stomach.

She could see Sloan's friends among the people, but not him. They'd flown in from Virginia and a host of new Redemption friends had made them welcome. Annie didn't know how she would have pulled everything together without those blessed, caring friends.

Kitty Wainright and Cheyenne Bowman had taken charge of the veranda for the reception. Kitty commandeered Jace Carter to help with the tables and if a few people noticed the tender looks passing from Jace to Kitty, they blamed the romantic mood of the day. Everyone knew the widowed Kitty would always mourn her soldier.

White linen cloths covered the tables set with a giant wedding cake made especially for the day by Miriam Martinelli down at the Sugar Shack. God bless the Martinellis. They'd worked for days on the luscious-looking creation. And both Sloan and Annie had agreed the day would not be true without clear glass jars of Aunt Lydia's lemonade and more jars of sweet tea to quench the thirst and bring the family history full circle.

"Annie." Her mother's voice turned her from the lace-bracketed windows. "It's almost time."

The news she'd wanted to hear jump-started her pulse. She giggled and the entourage crowded into the room laughed with her. So many smiles.

"Mama," she said softly, feeling the bittersweet moment. Her father wasn't here to give her away, but her heart had been Sloan's for so long, she'd decided to forgo that one tradition and simply go to him as she should have years ago. Tears threatened. Daddy wouldn't come home for a long time.

Her mother pulled her gently into an embrace. "Only tears

of joy are allowed today. The day you've dreamed of since you were sixteen."

She nodded, blinking back the moisture. Her mother had shown surprising strength during the weeks and months since the terrible confession. The town and church had wrapped their collective arms around her and helped her through this hardest of times. The wedding, Carleen claimed, was good for her. Planning had kept her too busy to think so much about the other. Still, Annie ached for her mother.

"You mess up that makeup and I'll hurt you." Jilly, her best friend and maid of honor, shoved a Kleenex into her hand. "No crying until after the pictures, you hear me?"

Annie retreated from her mother's hug with a watery smile. "Yes, boss."

Jilly was gorgeous today in a burnt-orange gown that set her red hair afire. Freckles and all, Annie thought she looked lovely.

She smoothed damp palms over her soft ruched and draped satin skirt of palest gold. She felt like a princess. No, not a princess. A blessed woman, beautiful because of the love filling her heart and soul. The pale gold gown was only window dressing.

From outside, she heard the faint strains of an acoustic guitar. "Oh. Oh." She waved nervous fingers in front of her.

Kitty Wainright poked her head through the door. "Time to rock and roll, ladies. Mrs. Crawford, your escort awaits."

Annie's brother, Neil, stood in the hall, crooked arm extended. Though he lived in Dallas, Neil had been coming home more often since their father's arrest. "Ready, Mom?"

Carleen's gaze met his and then swirled back to Annie. "You're the most beautiful bride I've ever seen." Tears filled her eyes.

"Stop, Mama." Annie rapidly fanned a hand in front of her

eyes. "You'll get me started again. Go. Take your rightful place as mother of the bride."

In a rustle of satin and lace, last-minute peeks in the mirror and a final hug, Carleen hooked her hand into her son's elbow and disappeared.

Delaney was next, as the only bridesmaid, dressed in a flowing burnt-orange gown identical to Jilly's. Her white-blond hair, held back by a pearl headband, fell softly around her shoulders. Holding a single, beribboned sunflower, she proudly followed her grandmother down the hall with Jilly close behind.

Then there was only Annie.

"Lord," she whispered. "Thank You." She knew God would understand all her heart held that words could not express.

Two ushers, wearing black tuxes and silly grins, swung wide the double French doors and Annie stepped out onto the veranda. "Jesu, Joy of Man's Desiring" swelled in joyous announcement over the gathering. She stood for a moment, soaking in the beautiful music and the Wedding Garden filled with friends and loved ones. Cameras flashed and snicked. She smiled and found the one her heart was reaching toward. He was there at the end of the pathway beneath the arbor, hands folded in front of him, waiting for her. She would finally be his. He would finally be hers. He smiled and the world, already bright with fall color and the spill of sunshine, seemed to glow.

There was Justin, too. Oh, my, he looked so grown-up and handsome, standing next to Mack Jett, Sloan's best man. She'd never seen her son prouder than the day Sloan had asked him to be his one and only groomsman.

They were stunning, all of them. Standing beneath the arbor with red and gold leaves rustling around them and the colors of the wedding blending with the season. Jilly and Delaney, Justin and Mack, with Pastor Parker between them.

But most of all—oh, most of all—her husband-to-be. In a black tux and a pale gold vest that matched her dress, with his black hair perfectly groomed and his blue eyes fastened on her, Sloan Hawkins was the handsomest man she'd ever seen.

"I love you," she mouthed, and his smile grew wider. He hitched his chin as if to say "Come on. I miss you."

Annie grinned and raised one eyebrow, then lifted the hem of her skirt and descended the steps to the path of autumn leaves scattered along the stone walkway.

Sloan had heard about this moment. The moment when a groom sees his bride coming toward him in her wedding finery. He'd never quite believed the stories, but now he did. Oh, man, did he ever!

His whole body reacted like a tuning fork, tuned especially to the melody that was Annie. His Annie. He thought maybe his heart really would fly out of his chest and go to Annie because it had always belonged with her in the first place.

She was a vision, her gown of palest gold shimmering in the sunlight, the perfect complement to pale hair and green, green eyes.

She stepped off the porch and started down the stone path, leaves dancing and whispering in joy against the flowing skirt. The path he and Justin, Jace and so many others had repaired and replaced to make this day as perfect as possible for Annie.

The trip was short but along the way she stopped for hugs and good wishes. When she reached Sloan, he murmured, "Took you long enough."

She laughed out loud and the wedding party chuckled. Sloan took her hand and tucked it into his folded elbow. A tingle of pure pleasure ran through him. Finally. He could hardly believe this day had come.

Pastor Parker, who had become a mentor and a friend,

began the ceremony in the traditional way. Sloan's heart beat so loudly, he wondered if he'd hear a word. And oh, how he wanted to treasure every word, every breath of this long-awaited day.

He focused on Annie as they repeated their vows, and was humbled by the light and love shining in her face. They exchanged rings with promises to love and honor one another with Christ as the center of their home. A few times they laughed. Several times they whispered "I love yous," and the unrehearsed moments of pure joy brought sighs and ahhs from the guests nearby.

At one point Sunny Case, in a pure soprano, sang "Give me Forever" and Sloan thought how perfect the words, because forever with Annie was all he wanted.

"Annie and Sloan," he heard the pastor say, "have chosen to close their ceremony in a special symbolic manner. Some of you may not be familiar with the salt covenant, so let me explain." He turned to a small altar behind him and retrieved a curving, elegant vase. "In Old Testament times, salt was very important and the salt covenant was a common, binding way of sealing an agreement. The symbolism is powerful. God says we are the salt of the earth. Salt mixed together cannot be separated, thus the covenant is unbreakable as marriage vows should also be unbreakable.

"Annie and Sloan, Delaney and Justin," he said, refocusing on them. "Each of you have individual vials of salt. Those vials symbolize your separate lives. They represent all that you are and all that you'll ever be as an individual. They also represent your lives before today. Four individuals who today are joined together as a family." He nodded to Sloan. "Sloan and Annie will now bring their vials."

Sloan slipped the tiny vial from his inner pocket and waited while Annie untied hers from a small ribbon on her bouquet, then handed her bouquet to a grinning Jilly. Pastor Parker held the pretty, curving vase where all could see. Together Sloan and Annie carefully emptied their vials into the waiting vase. As they did, Sloan felt the power of his promise to Annie. Like grains of salt mixed in a vase, their lives were forever joined.

"With this covenant," Sloan murmured the words they'd written together, "I join all that I am and all that I'll ever be with you. And with God as our guide and witness, nothing, *nothing* will ever separate us."

Heart in her eyes and fingers shaking just a bit, Annie repeated the words and emptied her vial with his. Sloan couldn't help himself. He took her fingers and kissed them.

"And now the children."

Sloan could hear the sniffles from the onlookers, and to tell the truth, he felt a little teary himself. With chest about to explode, he watched while his new son and daughter solemnly joined their lives to his.

A family. A real family. More than he'd ever dreamed possible. God was truly good and merciful.

"Just as these grains of salt can never be separated and poured again into the individual containers, so is your marriage a binding commitment, an unbreakable covenant of love." Pastor took the newly filled vase, capped it and set it on the table. "Now that you have pledged your lives together, it is my great and unique pleasure to pronounce you, Sloan, and you, Annie, husband and wife." Pastor Parker smiled at Sloan. "And as if you needed any encouragement, you may now kiss your bride."

Laughter and applause echoed over the garden as Sloan swept Annie into his arms and kissed her. Laughter bubbled up between them and he could practically feel Aunt Lydia and his mother looking on with tear-filled smiles.

"I love you, bride," he said, too thrilled to remember he was supposed to be walking her down the aisle.

"I love you, too, groom."

Two pairs of arms encircled them. Delaney and Justin. Heart full to overflowing, Sloan welcomed them into the circle. And there the four of them, the new family bound in love and covenant, looked into each other's eyes and laughed, bubbling over with love and happiness and the promise of tomorrow. For today—this blessed and beautiful day—God in his mercy and love had erased all the hurt and loneliness and had changed their mourning into joy.

* * * * *

Look for more books in RITA®-Award-winning author
Linda Goodnight's heartwarming miniseries
REDEMPTION RIVER,
where healing flows, coming in 2011!

Dear Reader,

Thank you for reading *The Wedding Garden,* book two in my new series, REDEMPTION RIVER. Sloan Hawkins is a special character, a hero I won't soon forget. He and his inner wounds arrived in my head fully developed and he insisted on having his story told. When a character really gets to me the way he did, I'm always a little sad to let him go when the book is finished. At the same time, I was glad to give Sloan his happy-ever-after with Annie and the children, though I shed a few tears on the journey. I hope you did, too.

I love hearing from my readers so feel free to contact me at Steeple Hill or through my website at:

www.lindagoodnight.com.

Thank you again for reading, and don't forget to meet me again in Redemption River, where healing flows.

Linda Goodnight

QUESTIONS FOR DISCUSSION

1. This book takes place in a fictional Oklahoma town founded during the Land Run of 1889. How did you envision the setting? How was it significant to the story?

2. Who is your favorite character in *The Wedding Garden?* Why? Describe him or her. What made that particular person stand out?

3. Who are the main characters? Did you like them? Could you empathize with them in any way? What are their issues?

4. Annie claims that Sloan has a skewed perception of his hometown. What did she mean? Do you agree?

5. The Wedding Garden is significant to the story both literally and symbolically. Discuss this significance, especially as it relates to Sloan's character.

6. Sloan believed the citizens of his hometown judged him for the sins of his father and mother. Did they? How did his perception affect his life, both past and present?

7. Aunt Lydia told Sloan that the truth would set him free. What did she mean? Was she correct? Is there a scripture reference for this?

8. There was great animosity between Sloan and Annie's father, Police Chief Dooley Crawford. Discuss some of the reasons for this hostility. Do you think Dooley's guilt had anything to do with his treatment of Sloan?

9. Sloan considered himself "a bad seed" because his father was a murderer. Is such a thing possible? Can a child bear the consequences for a parent's actions? How?

10. Did you suspect that Justin was Sloan's biological son? Do you think the revelation was handled realistically?

11. Justin is an angry boy. Why? Could Annie or Sloan have done anything more to help him heal? Did Sloan do the right thing by expecting Justin to work and pay for the broken windows?

12. *The Wedding Garden* is full of small town secrets. Discuss some of them. How did each dark secret affect the lives of the main characters?

13. Sloan says getting run out of town by Chief Dooley was the best and worst thing that could have happened to him. What does he mean?

Here's a sneak preview of
THE RANCHER'S PROMISE
by Jillian Hart.
Available in June 2010
from Love Inspired.

"So, are you back to stay?" Justin's deep voice hid any shades of emotion. Was he fishing for information or was he finally about to say "I told you so"?

"I'll probably go back to teaching in Dallas, but things could change. I'll just have to wait and see." The things in life she used to think were so important no longer mattered. Standing on her own two feet, building a life for herself, healing her wounds—that did.

"And this man you married?" he asked. "Did he leave you or did you leave him?"

"He threw me out." She waited for Justin's reaction. Surely a man with that severe a frown on his face was about to take delight in the irony. She'd turned down Justin's love, and her husband of five years had thrown away hers. If she were Justin, she would want her off his land.

"You were nothing but honest with me back then." He leaned against the railing, the wind raking his dark hair, and a different emotion passed across his hard countenance. "I was the one who never listened. I loved you so much, I don't think I could hear anything but what I wanted."

"I loved you, too. I wish I could have been different for you." Helpless, she took another step toward the driveway. She didn't know how to thank him. He could be treating her a lot worse right now, and she would deserve it. "Goodbye, Justin."

"I suppose you need a job?"

"I'll figure out something." Need a job? No, she was frantic for one. How did she tell him the truth?

Find out in THE RANCHER'S PROMISE.
Available June 2010 from Love Inspired.

Love Inspired®

Bestselling author

JILLIAN HART

brings you another heartwarming story
from

the
GRANGER
FAMILY
RANCH

Rancher Justin Granger hasn't seen his high school sweetheart
since she rode out of town with his heart. Now she's back, with
sadness in her eyes, seeking a job as his cook and housekeeper.
He agrees but is determined to avoid her…until he discovers
that her big dream has always been him!

The Rancher's Promise

*Available June
wherever books are sold.*

Steeple
Hill®

LI87601

LARGER-PRINT BOOKS!

**GET 2 FREE
LARGER-PRINT NOVELS
PLUS 2 FREE
MYSTERY GIFTS**

Love Inspired®

Larger-print novels are now available...

LILP10

Love Inspired®

TITLES AVAILABLE NEXT MONTH

Available May 25, 2010

THE RANCHER'S PROMISE
The Granger Family Ranch
Jillian Hart

RETURN TO ROSEWOOD
Rosewood, Texas
Bonnie K. Winn

COWBOY FOR KEEPS
Men of Mule Hollow
Debra Clopton

THE PASTOR TAKES A WIFE
Anna Schmidt

STEADFAST SOLDIER
Wings of Refuge
Cheryl Wyatt

THE HEART'S SONG
Winnie Griggs

LICNMBPA0510